RECLAIM

CASSIE LAELYN

COPYRIGHT 2021 by Cassie Laelyn

Title: Salvation

Author: Cassie Laelyn

Cover: Bookcoverology

Formatting: DL Gallie

Murder. Redemption. A love worth dying for.

When Kali Preston discovers her brother's death wasn't an accident, she resorts to desperate measures for help. Mainly, Brax Archer. The infuriatingly sexy, tattooed alpha of Cedar Valley bears. He's also the guy who tore out her heart and smashed it to pieces. But with a blood-thirsty killer targeting her family, evading Brax's sinful grin isn't her only danger.

Now, she must summon the strength to protect their pack before the hunter strikes again.

But what if those she loves are the biggest threat?

For you, for never letting go

chapter one

Kali

The familiar scent of chassis grease and dirty engine oil burned through my nose. Tools clanged almost in time with the heavy rock music thumping inside the garage. Usually, the combination soothed my soul. Not today.

I took a huge risk coming here.

Before I spoke, a big, brawny guy marched from the office toward me. "No way in Hell. Back that ass of yours out the door."

Instead of cowering and retreating, I planted my feet to the ground. "I'm here to see Brax."

This guy's size would scare the pants off anyone. But not me. Underneath all the bulk and muscle, I just hoped he was a caring, cuddly teddy bear. A tattoo-covered, scruffy teddy bear with tree-trunk sized arms.

They existed, right?

Imagining this guy as a squishy teddy didn't stop my pulse from shooting through the roof. Especially as two other guys with similar beefy builds closed in from either side. A third abandoned his search in a fire-engine red toolbox to stand with his arms crossed over his bulky chest, scowling at me. That guy was even taller.

I refused to let them intimidate me. I'd come too far to back out now.

I answered their glares with one of my own and straightened my shoulders. "I know he's here."

Without slowing his stride, Teddy Bear clutched my upper arm in a firm grip, spun me around, and strode me out the door. Confidence was no match for sheer strength. The brisk fall wind caught my breath. Crunchy, dried leaves tumbled along the sidewalk, swirling around my boots.

He released my arm and stood in front of me. Towering over me is more accurate. The guy was huge.

Thanks to the sewn letters on the breast pocket of Teddy Bear's navy coveralls, I at least knew his name. "Rhett, I'm not leaving until I see him."

Rhett ripped the baseball cap off his head and huffed a deep, rather annoyed breath. "He's not here. You shouldn't be here either."

I knew that. Everyone knew that. If I had another option, I would've taken it.

"I need you to call him. Tell him Kali's here."

"I know who you are." Rhett's ice-blue eyes narrowed. "Why should I? So he goes through the pain of leaving his family all over again? 'Cause I can tell you now, that shit wasn't fun to watch the first time."

This wouldn't be easy. Brax went to great lengths to exile himself from his family. Ever since my brother...

I shook my head, clearing the nightmare from my mind. Now wasn't the time to relive that.

Hoping contact tugged on Rhett's big teddy bear emotions, I touched his arm. "Please. It's really important."

His brows smoothed as his expression softened. Minutes passed as he stood there, looking at me, searching for something. What? No idea. But whatever he found made him huff another breath. He slipped the baseball cap back on his head. Just when I thought he'd turn and walk away, he grabbed a cell from his back pocket.

"I'll text him," he muttered, thumbs tapping on the screen. "Whether he comes is up to him."

I nodded because words couldn't form with the giant lump taking up residence in my throat.

Biting the inside of my lip, I waited. We both waited. Rhett stood there in silence like a bodyguard, ready to maul anyone who messed with him. He was a shifter but I couldn't tell which animal.

In the background, the other three guys resumed working. Tools clanged, and the music blared through the open doorway. One guy bellowed the lyrics. Hopefully, he was a better mechanic than singer. Cars cruised back and forth down the main street, while a handful of people strolled past us on the sidewalk without a care in the world. I envied them.

Rhett was clearly more comfortable with silence than me. Only his eyes moved, continually darting this way and that. Meanwhile, my whole body buzzed, wired with energy. Every nerve ending crackled, and my heart pounded. Low in my gut, a swarm of butterflies attempted to burst free from their enclosure.

Would he come? Would he face me? Did I want him to? With equal proportions, I'd dreaded this reunion and ached for it more than my next breath.

I had no idea how long we stood there waiting. It could've been three minutes, but it felt like freaking hours. Rhett's phone finally pinged, making my heart leap. Half of me wanted to bounce from foot to foot, while the other half wanted to keel over and hurl.

Rhett palmed the phone and swore under his breath.

Good sign or bad?

Without replying to the text, he shoved the cell back in his pocket. "The universe is on your side. He's across the street."

"What?" Air punched from my lungs so fast it made me dizzy. "As in this street?"

Before Rhett answered, I spotted a guy weaving through the afternoon crowd at the bar across the road, heading out the door to the sidewalk. My chest squeezed so tight it may never inflate again.

Rhett mumbled something, but I couldn't comprehend the words. All necessary brain function diverted to the guy wearing dark blue ripped jeans, a short sleeve black t-shirt teamed with a full sleeve of ink down one arm, and a familiar black baseball cap. Brax Archer. Bear shifter, rightful alpha of Cedar Valley, and the guy who officially smashed my heart.

Brax stood on the sidewalk across the road, and his gaze locked with mine. My skin tingled and danced, and my stupid heart ached more than ever. He was still a picture-perfect specimen of alpha male. Why was life so cruel?

Two cars cruised down the street, and he just waited for them to pass, in no hurry to cross the road. Which was totally fine. At a distance, I could stare at him for eternity. The problem was never the way his deep brown eyes caused every inch of my body to ignite. All the other emotions wedged between us caused the pain.

The traffic lights at one end of the street turned red. That lump in my throat doubled in size. With his intense gaze still fixed on me, Brax crossed the road with long, confident strides, not dashing to beat the traffic lights. If they turned green before he reached the other side, he probably expected the cars to swerve around him.

Smug shit.

The closer he came, the more I second-guessed my decision to involve him. The more my fist ached to connect with his god-like jaw.

Why the hell did I come here?

The moment Brax reached my side of the sidewalk, I swear I stopped breathing. My heart raced so fast the Sheriff might issue a ticket.

Rhett squeezed Brax's shoulder. "Want me to stay?"

Still staring at me, Brax shook his head.

Rhett turned his attention to me, giving a pained expression somewhere between, "You hurt him again and I'll find you," and "He's been lost without you."

Clearly, Brax hadn't told Rhett the full story. But sure, whatever, blame me.

Instead of unpacking all those feelings, I murmured a thank you. Rhett gave a curt nod before returning inside the garage, this time closing the door.

Now what the hell did I do? What did I say to the man who I'd loved more than life itself before he upped and disappeared?

Without a damn word, Brax clutched my arm and marched me back inside the garage.

Ferocity erupted from deep inside me, and I shoved out of his grasp. "You know what, I'm over being man-handled today."

Brax's body went deadly still, so close I felt power and rage vibrating off his shoulders. Black flashed in his eyes as his bear fought for control. A low growl rumbled from his chest. He inched closer, and I lifted my chin to maintain eye contact.

"Who the fuck man-handled you?"

His tone left no doubt that if he found out who it was, he'd shred them to bits in two seconds flat. From the corner of my eye, Rhett gravitated closer. Regardless of Rhett's animal, this would end in a fight. What I didn't need was more death in my life.

Maybe man-handled was a slight exaggeration.

I sighed, hoping it diffused some of the tension in Brax. It didn't. "Besides you just now?"

Brax ripped off his baseball cap and dragged a hand

through his disheveled black hair. "Shit. I didn't mean... Sorry, Kal." His eyes faded back to their natural deep brown shade as his bear retreated, no longer sensing a threat. "Seeing you here is..."

"Hard. I get it. It's hard for me, too, but you don't see me shoving people around."

Brax nodded, and without the man-handling this time, ushered me into an office at the rear of the garage, closing the door behind us.

I couldn't sit. In the confined space his earthy pine scent consumed my senses and muddled my damn thoughts. Instead, I stood behind a ratty old armchair. In the far corner of the office, I spotted Brax's duffle bag and some folded linen.

He leaned his butt against the cluttered desk, cap back on his head, hands shoved into his pockets. "Why are you here?"

"Seriously? That's the first thing you say to me after two years?"

His lips thinned. "What do you want me to ask, Kal? How have you been? Are you happy? Are you seeing someone? 'Cause I really don't wanna know the answers."

Seeing him again was harder than I expected. So much. To be fair, I didn't want him to answer those questions either. Ripping off the Band-Aid should've been the less painful option. It wasn't. I still wasn't even sure if I wanted to see him again after the shitty move he pulled on me.

Did I blame him for leaving? Absolutely. Kind of. No, not really. Because without being in his position, I couldn't say how I would've reacted. Maybe I would've done the same. And knowing that irritated me even more.

Instead of answering those painful questions, I grabbed the cell from my back pocket, opened a text message I received three days ago, and showed him. "This is why I'm here."

"Fuck." Brax stared at the message. The muscles in his jaw tightened, working overtime.

"Is it true? Or some sick prank?"

His gaze dragged back to me.

"I dunno."

I studied his expression, the slight flare of his nostrils, the way his brows bunched together in a tight, angry line. He was furious, no doubt about it, but he didn't seem shocked. I'd nearly collapsed when I first read it. Him... not at all. "You don't seem surprised."

He waited a few seconds before answering. "I got the same message."

"What?"

He pulled out his cell, tapped on the screen, then held it facing me.

"Three days ago, I got the same message, from the same number."

"And you never thought to tell me?" My voice rose as a wild, bubbly mess of emotions exploded. "I didn't abandon everyone, Brax. Not like you. You knew where I was, you could've told me about the text. You could've... come home."

"It's my job to protect you. Which includes not involving you in shit I've got under control."

I threw my hands in the air. "Protect me? You left me."

Coming here was a mistake. I couldn't be here any longer. The familiar smells, Brax touching me, my anger at him for leaving. It all became too much.

I shoved the phone back into my pocket. "I came here as a courtesy, Brax. Not to ask your permission. I'm investigating this with or without your help."

Brax gripped the edge of the desk so hard his knuckles bulged. "Go back to Cedar Valley. I'll call you when I find something."

"No." I made my own decisions, not him. How dare he push me aside. "I'm not leaving until I figure out who killed my brother."

chapter two

Brax

Kali Preston spun and stormed out the office door, not giving me the chance to explain. Not that I blamed her. What the hell would I even say? I could've called her or drove back home. Hell, I could've even called one of my brothers. Harley always had a soft spot for Kali. He could've acted as the link between us and kept Kali in the loop.

I received the same text at the same time but was too much of a coward to face her.

Why? I didn't know. Dredging up those memories wasn't something I looked forward to, even less than the thought of facing Kali's disappointment. Not a day went by when I didn't think of her, but that didn't mean all the pain between us magically disappeared. It still hung on like a leech, sucking the essence out of me minute by minute. And her coming here just gave that sucker a burst of life.

I barely made it through leaving her last time. If she wriggled her way back into my life again, I wouldn't survive a repeat. She was better off far away from me.

Cementing my feet to the ground, I stood in the doorway as Kali cut across the garage. I didn't call out to her or shout above the too-loud music. Instead, I stood there and let her walk away from me this time.

Beside the hoist, Rhett glared at me, but I didn't give a shit. Kali shouldn't be here, and not just because I couldn't deal with seeing her again. I'd promised her brother I'd protect her and being near me wasn't safe.

When Kali barged through the garage door and out onto the sidewalk, I thought I'd breathe a sigh of relief. Only, I didn't. My stupid black heart sparked to life earlier when I caught sight of her from across the street and now familiar, unwanted, or more accurately, unwarranted, feelings soared back to the surface.

Counting to fifty, I waited until a car started outside and drove away before I headed to the door.

"You just gonna let her go?"

Rhett crossed his arms over his chest and frowned at me.

Why the hell was everyone on Team Kali? "Yep. Exactly the plan. I've got this under control. There's no reason to involve her."

I'd already put out some feelers about who could've sent the text and whether it was bullshit. Hunters hadn't threatened Cedar Valley since...Well, since *that* night. The sender was probably some dipshit from a neighboring pack trying to stir up trouble.

"She got the text too, didn't she? That's why she came here."

When I didn't answer, Rhett kept fucking talking.

"Then why did you send her away?"

"She's better off going back home where it's safe."

Rhett cocked a brow. "Is that for her benefit or yours?"

Both our benefits. But saying that only gave Rhett more ammunition. Before I settled here in Timber Falls, I'd wandered the countryside for a good six months after leaving Cedar Valley, wondering what the hell I should do. Rhett interrogated me for a solid week before granting me permission to remain in his town. I would've done the same in the reversed situation. It wasn't every day an alpha walked away from their pack and lived in another shifter community.

Leaving hurt like a bitch, but I deserved nothing less.

"For fuck's sake, Rhett, just drop it."

Just because Rhett was the alpha of the Timber Falls wolves, it didn't mean I'd let him question the decisions I made for my town, regardless of whether I still lived there or not.

"Listen," Rhett held up his palm, "I don't often disagree with your choices, and I never question why you don't return home. But leaving was a shitty move. I know it, and you know it."

Memories flashed through my mind, making my bear stir again, harder this time.

"Calm the fuck down," Rhett snapped. "The last thing I need is a grizzly clawing all the fucking cars to bits. Insurance doesn't cover pissed-off bears."

Inhaling a few deep breaths, I clenched and unclenched my fists while sending a mental message to my bear that I had things under control. Well, in the garage. Gradually, my grizzly retreated to his slumber state.

Rhett's shoulders relaxed. "I figured you didn't tell me the full story about what happened between the two of you, but if she got that text, too, she's already involved. Look at what happened the other month in Woodland Falls. Hunters have become bolder, targeting more packs and not giving a shit about the carnage. No one's safe. Are you willing to let one of your pack snoop around on their own? Without protection? Because regardless of whether you're in Cedar Valley or not, that bear pack is still yours."

Rhett was right. Kali wouldn't let this go. Between her and Zac, Kali got the stubborn gene. She wouldn't sit on the sidelines and wait for updates from me. She wouldn't be satisfied until she interrogated every goddamn person living in a hundred-mile radius. Searching for answers put herself, Rhett's pack, and Cedar Valley in more danger. No thanks to an ancient clan of witches who decided centuries ago to turn themselves into bloodthirsty shifter hunters. We already had big enough targets on our backs. We always would. Kali didn't need to draw more attention by snooping around.

"Damn it." I ripped my truck keys out of my pocket. "I need to skip work for a few days."

"Brax, you're the best damn mechanic I ever had in this shop, but I knew you staying here was only temporary. Go do what you need to do. Call if you need back-up."

"I'll be back when it's sorted."

The torn expression on Rhett's face nearly undid me. Kali coming here changed everything. For her, my pack, and for me.

"We'll see."

Before anyone changed their mind, mainly me, I packed my gear, grabbed my duffle bag, and left.

With only two motels in Timber Falls, it wasn't hard to track down Kali. I pulled into the motel parking lot next to her car. Calling this place a dive was an understatement. Even the neon sign on the roof had seen better days, with half the lights not working and letters missing. After they built the interstate, the only tourists were those seeking an escape from the city to connect with the wilderness. They were few and far between these days.

Sleeping at the garage was better than this. A makeshift bed on a cold concrete floor at the rear of the office wasn't ideal, but it sure as shit kept memories at bay. It also prevented me from putting down roots in a town I'd never call home. Only one place was home to me, and I wasn't welcome back there.

Getting out of the truck, I stood in the parking lot for a moment to steady my breath. I hadn't seen Kali in two years. Two fucking years. In that time my heart never stopped aching, begging me to go back. The day would come when she found me, I knew that, but I'd hoped it was under better circumstances. Preferably after I got my shit together and could offer her more than an apology.

After sweet-talking the receptionist for Kali's room number, I took my time ascending the metal staircase, giving my stupid brain a chance to figure out a way to not involve Kali. No such luck. My brain rarely worked with her around. And that twisted part of me wanted to keep her close even if she hated me.

At the door, I raised my hand to knock, but it opened before I had the chance.

Kali stood just inside the doorway, hazel eyes narrowed, and for a second I lost myself in memories. This was a bad idea.

"If you're here to tell me to leave again, you're wasting your time."

My pulse was all over the joint, beating so erratically the rush of blood echoed in my ears. Kali hadn't changed one bit in the time we'd been apart. Though she looked older, wiser somehow. Matured with life experience. Being Zac's little sister, I'd always kept my distance, denied the pull between us, until that one night when I finally acknowledged she was my mate. The same night my world fucking fell apart.

"Brax?"

"Sorry." I shoved those memories back in their box and locked it tight. Fucking padlocked it. Wrapped it with explosives in case I tried to open it again. Inhaling, I locked my gaze with hers. "I'll help you."

"Why?"

A thousand reasons why. So afterward I could drive

her ass back to Cedar Valley and make sure she stayed there under my family's protection. So I could return to hiding in a small-town garage, ignoring all my screw-ups. Or better yet, so I could keep pretending I hadn't failed her.

None of those reasons made it out of my mouth.

"It's not safe to snoop around on your own."

Hands flung to her hips. "I'm not sitting in a motel room waiting for you to drip feed me information. You forget, I know you, Brax Archer. Pushing me aside isn't protecting me."

I softened my voice so she'd stop biting off my head. "We'll work together."

Working together would hurt like hell. But finding out who killed Zac was our priority. Once we got to the bottom of it, we could both go our separate ways.

I stepped closer, shoving my hands in my pockets so I didn't reach out and tuck that loose strand of hair behind her ear.

"Zac was my best friend. He was a brother to me. I need this as much as you do."

Her eyes shone with an emotion I was all too familiar with. My fingers burned to comfort her, to ease the pain somehow. But just like every other guy in this town, I had no right. Not anymore.

Besides, nothing dulled the pain of losing your only sibling.

Blinking back tears, she nodded. "Okay."

Kali was stubborn, but she was also smart. One crisis averted.

"Good." I grabbed the duffle I'd stashed by the door out of sight.

Kali's eyes widened, shooting between me and the bag.

"Wait a minute. What do you think you're doing?"

The way her voice hitched made me growl. I used to love throwing her off guard, especially when she'd playfully swat at me. But that was before…

Nope, not going there. Thinking of Kali in that way only made it harder once this was over.

Instead, I slipped past her into the room. "Moving in."

chapter three

Kali

I stood there dumbfounded as Brax strode into the motel room despite my objections. He dumped his duffle on the small round table. His bag thumped, and I expected the table to collapse in a heap. The chair almost did when I sat on it earlier.

I was no woman of luxury, but the motel seriously needed a major refurbishment.

"You can't stay here, Brax."

He scanned the tiny room, ducked his head into the bathroom before he pulled out a chair, flipped it around, and sat on it backward. "I made a vow to Zac that I intend to keep until the day I die. I won't risk your safety by having you stay here alone and unprotected."

"There you go again. You and your vows. How can you believe you protected me by leaving?"

He flinched. "I didn't leave you *unprotected*, Kal."

"Oh, right. I guess that was in the fine print."

Sure, I wasn't unprotected, but I didn't want protection from his family or other shifters. All I wanted was for him to come home. Living without Zac was hard enough. Losing the other half of my heart straight afterward almost killed me.

Brax wasn't only my protector. He was my best friend. The guy I wanted to grow old with. The guy who stamped his name on my heart long before Zac died.

"What if I shifted for the first time and there was no one to help me?"

His back straightened. "Did you?"

The concern in his voice made my heart bleed. "No. But I could have."

He relaxed again, crossing his forearms along the back of the chair. "I want you to live a normal life, Kal. We have no idea if both your parents were shifters. For all we know, one of them could've been human. In that case, there's only a fifty-fifty chance you'll be one of us. Stop hoping for something that should've happened by now."

One of us.

That hurt. Like, really hurt. Did he have to be so blunt?

"Zac was a bear," I countered, my heart tearing apart for a whole new reason.

"Doesn't mean you will be."

And there he was, stating the obvious. That festered wound ripped open, spurting blood and gore on the dirty olive-green motel walls. Springs creaked as I sank onto the corner of the bed. Acknowledging I should stop hoping for something that should've happened by now and actually doing it were two totally different things. "Sometimes I think I don't belong anywhere."

"Just because you never knew your mother and you had a screwed-up father, doesn't mean you don't belong anywhere. I don't care if you're not a shifter, Kal. I've always told you that. It doesn't matter to me. I will...the Archer pack will always be your family. Cedar Valley is your home. That's where you belong."

In my heart, I knew that. I *felt* it. Cedar Valley just didn't feel like home without Brax.

My phone pinged with a text and I grabbed it from the nightstand, reading it before turning to Brax. "Levi said he contacted his buddy and he'll try to trace the number."

Brax threw his hands in the air. "What the hell? You told Levi?"

"He's your brother, remember? Not the enemy. Plus, he has a buddy on the force which, so far, is our only lead."

Brax ripped off his baseball cap and twisted it between his hands. "The more people who know about this, the harder it is to contain. I suppose you told Harley, too?"

I nodded. "He was with me when I got the text."

"Of course he fucking was." He raked his fingers

through his hair. "I don't want them involved. What I want is for you to check out of this shit-box and go home where it's safer. But I know you're too stubborn to let this go."

I recoiled. "Let it go? Zac was my brother. After two years, someone sent us both a text saying that his death wasn't an accident like we all first thought, and you want me to let this go? What if it was Levi who died? Would you let that go? What if it wasn't a random human passing through town? What if it was a hunter and they're still out there, targeting the pack?"

He paused a moment, staring at me. Dread churned in my stomach. I knew that look. The last time I'd seen it was right before he left town and never came back.

He slipped on the baseball cap and stood. "This is a bad idea."

"Are you serious?" I matched his stance and raised the stakes with a glare. "I came here asking for your help. Don't you dare walk out on me again."

His eyes narrowed. Without knowing what else to say, I bit my tongue and waited. Brax was always better at battling his demons in silence. But the silence made it worse for me. Each moment we didn't speak, memories drifted to the front of my mind, and my heart ached a little more. Once the ache dimmed, it morphed into a shitload of resentment and anger. He didn't just walk out on me, he left his family and started a whole new life here as though no one in his past ever existed. I wouldn't let him do that to me again.

The flicker of emotion in his eyes retreated behind his perfectly erected walls. My chest squeezed.

Without another word, Brax strode out the door, slamming it closed behind him.

———

Half an hour later, after a childish meltdown followed by a shower, I flopped onto the bed and stared at the ceiling. I was so stupid. Coming here was a long shot. I should've known Brax wouldn't help.

But I thought he would at least care about his brothers.

Stretching my arm to the right, I snatched my cell and checked for an update from Levi. Nothing. I sighed and dropped it back on the bed. Everything was fine. I could do this without Brax. Once I got out of my funky mood, I'd decide on Plan B. First up, I'd return to the garage and speak to Rhett. He seemed like the guy in charge, maybe even the local alpha. I sucked at sensing those things. Probably because I wasn't *one of them*. After that, I'd come up with the next step.

The door swung open. I jolted upright, almost falling off the bed. Brax strode in, a pizza box in one hand, a six-pack of beer in the other. A growly look on his face. Sexy, but not entirely friendly. Near freezing air rushed into the motel room after him.

Using the heel of his boot, he kicked the door shut. "Do you ever lock the door?"

I scowled at him, then slid off the bed to flip the lock in an exaggerated, pissed-off manner. When I turned around, Brax popped the cap off two beers and handed me one.

"I thought you left."

He swigged his beer before he sat and opened the pizza box. "I told you I'd help. Plus, why would I leave my bag here if I wasn't coming back?" He dipped his chin at the duffle bag now on the floor in the corner.

Good point.

"I just needed...a moment."

He wasn't the only one. Controlling my emotions was the key around Brax. Maybe then my investigation skills would improve.

I took a long draft of my beer. When the spicy scent of grilled pepperoni made my stomach growl, I caved and joined him at the small table.

Brax cleared his throat, lightly chipping away at the label on his beer. "Did you reply to the text?"

Staying focused on the task was a smart idea. We should avoid discussing the gigantic black hole front and center between us. Once we found out who killed Zac, I'd return to Cedar Valley and let Brax carry on living his new responsibility-free life.

"No. Did you?"

He shook his head before swigging the beer. Picked the label. Repeat. Little bits of torn paper piled on the table in front of him.

"Harley said it's probably some sick joke. That if a shifter hunter had killed Zac, they wouldn't have stopped at him. They would've attacked the whole pack that night. He's still adamant it was a human and that the text was sent by some idiot wanting to cause pack drama."

"Maybe." He gave a half-hearted shrug.

Not exactly a convincing answer. "I'd rather know for sure though, wouldn't you?"

He nodded. "How d'you know I was in Timber Falls?" He grabbed a slice of pizza, folded it in his hand, and took a bite.

His tone wasn't angry or accusing me of doing something wrong. It wasn't even surprised. More resigned to the fact I'd find him eventually, so he changed the conversation to a less dangerous topic. Small talk was usually my specialty.

Now, though, it pissed me off. If he hadn't left, I wouldn't have needed to find him. We'd be living the life I always imagined. His brothers wouldn't be working stupid hours picking up the slack at their garage. The Archer ranch would feel like a home again.

But he did leave. He made the choice to desert his family. To leave...me.

I stuffed another bite of pizza in my mouth and chewed as slowly as I could, so I didn't snap his head off. "Levi tracked the money you sent every month. In-person deposits at a bank are easy to trace, apparently."

He held my gaze while finishing his mouthful.

I didn't wait. If we were asking hard questions, I had a few of my own.

"Why did you leave?"

He snatched his beer and chugged before clunking it back on the table. "Let's agree on some ground rules."

"Okaaay."

"No dredging up the past. Leave that shit in the past where it belongs."

I nodded, and he kept speaking.

"And stop passing information to my brothers. The fewer people involved, the better."

I nodded again, though somehow Brax made all the ground rules and gave me no say in the matter. Screw that. "Fine. But you promise to involve me in everything. Don't gloss over something because you think it's protecting me. I came to you, remember. Don't shove me aside."

The muscles in his jaw tightened like crazy, and black flashed in his pupils. "Fine. But I have one more condition."

My stomach churned. "What?"

His hard gaze narrowed, leaving no room for miscommunication.

"Once we figure out who killed Zac, you'll return to Cedar Valley."

Alone.

He hadn't said it, but I knew he silently tacked on the word. "Fine."

chapter four

Brax

After our awkward-as-fuck pizza and beers, I settled into the armchair by the door while Kali changed in the bathroom. If anyone busted in, this gave me the perfect position to claw the shit out of them. Plus, the chair was better than a cold concrete floor at the garage. And a hell of a lot less uncomfortable than addressing the issue of only one bed in the room.

When Kali dashed from the bathroom to the bed wearing a pair of sleep shorts and a tank top, I tried not to look. Glimpsing all that bare skin stirred parts of my body I needed to ignore when around her. Responding to them, or even acknowledging they existed, was a bad idea. Instead, I stared at the ceiling until she tucked herself into bed, burying herself beneath the covers. Only then did I permit my eyes to drift lower. To the wall.

"Thanks for grabbing dinner," Kali murmured, snuggling further under the bedding. It'd cover her head in a minute.

I grunted. Getting pizza gave me an opportunity to calm down. Being near Kali wired my bear like nothing else. I needed to figure out how to make her go back to Cedar Valley. The longer she stayed here with me, the harder it would be to leave her again.

"Get some sleep, Kal. In the morning we'll figure out a plan."

She nodded, though the slight narrowing of her eyes told me loud and clear she wasn't happy I cut off any further conversation. The sick, twisted part of me hoped she'd argue, get all growly at me.

Fuck. I needed to sort my shit out and stop thinking of her like that. We could never happen. Not after what I did.

Kali rolled onto her side, facing away from me. I switched off the lamp and stretched out on the uncomfortable chair, crossing my arms over my chest. Not exactly a perfect sleeping position.

My mind wouldn't shut the hell up. I thought staying in the same room as her would be fine, that we could put the past aside while we figured out what really happened to Zac. Something that had haunted me for two long years.

It should've been me. Not Zac.

Kali's scent, the smell of her perfume, the smell of her hair, the sound of her fucking voice made me crazy. And that was before my bear caught a whiff of her. Ever since, my grizzly had clawed inside my head like a caged feral animal desperate to break free. Letting my bear loose was a dumbass move and something that would get me in shit with Rhett's wolf pack. Rhett and I'd come to an agreement when I arrived. I only let my grizzly out deep in the mountains—away from humans, and off the wolf reservation. My bear had sulked for the past few months refusing to shift, so I stopped bothering. Now, he made up for it, and the timing couldn't be worse.

"Will you lie with me?"

I froze. My pulse flipped around like crazy. All internal thoughts ceased.

She whispered the words so softly, maybe I imagined it. Wouldn't be the first time. Only this time, Kali was here in the same room, not a memory or figment of my imagination. Was that any easier?

If I didn't acknowledge her, then I wouldn't have to answer or admit how much I ached to hear those words.

Lying in the same bed with her was too risky, even if we were both fully clothed. Having her body near mine would throw me over the edge. I'd craved it for too long. Like a kid holding a firecracker, inching it closer and closer to the flame until it exploded the whole fucking sky. That would happen. Every cell in my body would incinerate.

"Just until I fall asleep," she added, rolling over to face the center of the bed.

Goddamn it.

I guess I could lie on the bed for a bit. Just until she fell asleep. It couldn't hurt. Then I'd go back to the chair. We'd done that plenty of times as kids when she was scared or upset. Nothing else ever happened. This time would be no different.

With that fucked up logic, I crawled on top of the covers on the opposite side of the bed and lay facing her, my head propped up by my hand. That way I wouldn't accidentally fall asleep, nor would my hands assume a mind of their own and wander toward her.

The bed was far comfier than the chair. When was the last time I got a decent night's sleep? The garage floor had nothing on an actual bed with linen and shit.

After I settled in, Kali closed her eyes. She remained silent for so long that I assumed she'd drifted off. Her breathing settled, and funnily enough, so did mine. A familiar sense of calm washed through my blood, a feeling I only ever experienced around her. My bear reacted the same. Mentally curling up next to her, he settled into a deep slumber. A fated mate always affected their other half this way. Calmed. Grounded. I'd been without that peace for so damn long.

"I don't blame you for Zac's death." Kali's eyes fluttered open.

The hurt behind them ripped a new gash inside my damn soul.

"I never got a chance to tell you that."

It didn't matter. I blamed myself. The lump in my throat returned with a vengeance.

She paused, seeming to find the right words. "I think

we all blame ourselves for what could've been. If we weren't..."

I'd never been so glad for someone to leave a sentence unfinished. Tonight wasn't the right time to unpack our past. Maybe in a hundred years. Next millennia perhaps. Not now. Not in the middle of the night, in a shitty motel room, lying beside her for the first time in two years.

"Why won't you talk to me? We used to talk about everything and then one day...nothing."

More proof lying on the bed was a reckless idea. "No bringing up the past, remember? Try to get some sleep."

Asshole move. But I couldn't do this right now.

Her eyes searched mine. Dim light filtered in the room from around the window drapes, making the flecks of gold in her eyes shimmer.

My hand betrayed me. It reached out and brushed a strand of hair from her face, tucking it behind her ear. Kali exhaled a soft breath, angling her cheek to my touch. How easy it was to touch her. To lose myself in the comfort and security of having her close. For a split second, I almost forgot how her brother's death wasn't only my worst failure but also led to my biggest regret.

Kali's eyes closed for a moment and reopened all glassy. The gaping hole inside my heart widened, expanding so much it added a whole new dimension to the pain.

I should've been there for her. I shouldn't have left. But I didn't deserve to stay.

"Go to sleep. I'll be here when you wake."

That was all I could offer. Her eyes slid closed again,

and within minutes, her breathing steadied to a soft, even rhythm.

I rolled onto my back and locked my hands under my head so I stopped touching her. My bear still snoozed, happy to be in the same vicinity as Kali. Bastard. Wish it was that easy for me.

When in bear form, my mind slept while my grizzly took over, but on the change back, memories flashed through my head. Just enough to relive my damn bear wandering a step behind Kali protecting her from hidden threats. Or reliving the feel of her petting his fur. Kali's love for my bear caused a hot jealous rage at every shift. I wanted that with her. I wanted her to love me like she did my bear. But she didn't deserve a screwed-up, failed alpha. Fated mate or not.

The motel room ceiling was just as shitty from this angle. Boring, dirty, and stained with something I didn't want to know. Perfect combination for sending my mind into la-la land. My eyes grew heavy. My breathing steadied.

Kali's cell phone rang on the nightstand. We jolted upright at the same time and shot out of bed.

"Hello?" Her voice was groggy with sleep.

I stood at the opposite side of the bed while she spoke in the handset. "Who is it?"

She held her palm up, shushing me. The fuck she did.

"Sorry, Levi. What did you say?"

Just great. Levi. My kid brother. He and Kali were the same age, and they'd gone to high school together. He made her laugh like no other.

So not getting jealous right now.

"Yeah, he's here with me," she said to Levi.

I flicked on a lamp and paced in a tight circle. Not like the room was big enough for a large circle. I could barely dry myself in the bathroom let alone do laps.

"No. Tell me what's going on," she snapped, suddenly awake and cranky as hell.

Her face looked ready to explode. Hand gripped tight around the cell, her lips formed the thinnest line. Any thinner and they'd become one.

"Stop treating me like a helpless child."

She paused where I assumed Levi gave as good as he got from Kali. Those two had that solid brother/sister relationship where they fought like territorial bears one minute, then hung out like best friends the next. Always had.

"Ugh! Fine."

The pacing ended in an abrupt halt when Kali threw the cell at me. Fine, she didn't throw it at me. She hurled it at the bed so hard it bounced off the mattress and thudded on the floor in front of my feet.

I picked it up and stared at the screen. I hadn't spoken to my brothers since I left. Two years disconnected from my family. Back home, they pissed me off daily, living in the same house did that to brothers, but I'd never gone more than twenty-four hours without seeing one of them. Then all at once, my life imploded.

"It's Levi," Kali snapped, jerking her chin to the cell in my hand.

I stared at it some more. What the hell was wrong

with me? Holding that little device up to my ear seemed like the hardest fucking task.

"He won't tell me what's going on. Something happened. Of course, he'd talk to you. Everyone forgets that you left. I'm the one who got the text. I'm the one who came to find you...Brax?" She raised her voice. "Are you even listening?"

Yes. No. "What did you say?"

Kali growled at me. Actually growled. So damn proud of her.

"Put the phone to your ear."

Okay, I could do this. Speaking wasn't that difficult. On the other end of the cell was my brother. I could...

"Brax!"

"All right!" Phone to ear. "Yeah?"

"What took you so long? I thought Kali must've thrown the phone or something." Levi snorted.

I don't know why I thought things would be different. Three in the morning and Levi laughed on the phone as though I'd seen him only yesterday.

"What happened?" I wanted to ask what was so urgent that it couldn't wait until morning. And why he wouldn't tell Kali. Must be bad.

Kali threw her hands in the air and huffed. For a second I couldn't take my eyes off her. Earlier, I glimpsed the same sleepwear from the other side of the room but diverted my gaze to the ceiling because it didn't feel right. Neither did now, though I lacked the same level of restraint.

Every part of my body awoke at the sight, and I couldn't prevent the wicked images from coming to life in my brain. I imagined her soft skin under my hands, my fingers trailing down the curve of her waist before settling on her hips. A sweet ache swelled through my middle. With her back to me, she slipped on a pair of sweatpants before gathering her golden-brown hair into a loose bun at the nape of her neck. For a long moment, she stared at the carpet, seeming to compose herself, before she turned around and caught me watching like a fucking creeper. I didn't look away. Part of me wanted her to catch me. I wanted her to see how much she affected me.

Her eyes softened, the earlier fight in them diminished. Her pretty, full lips parted.

Reasoning kicked in and slapped me in the goddamn face. Old feelings were a bitch. I couldn't go there.

Not bringing up the past was smart, but that didn't prevent the memories from slamming against that cage while they attempted to escape. Instead, I tightened the motherfucking lock. I couldn't hurt her again. I wouldn't.

Just as Kali opened her mouth to speak, the solo conversation happening on the other end of the phone snapped my attention.

"What the fuck did you just say?" I said into the handset.

"Someone slaughtered a wolf and sprayed the blood all over the garage door."

Receiving a text was one thing, but a direct threat to my family? That was a whole other level. Knowing this latest information sent my bear into a frenzy. He practically clawed at the inside of my skull like a raging lunatic.

Kali must've noticed my expression or how I gripped the cell so tight it almost cracked.

"Brax?"

She rounded the bed to stand before me.

"What is it?"

"Hey, bro? You still there?" Levi asked.

Answering Levi first was the easier option. How the hell would I tell Kali? "Yeah, I'm here. Any rogue shifters been on the property?"

"Nope."

Dread sank low and heavy in my gut. "Any packs report a missing wolf?"

"Not that I know of. Harley's gonna make some calls."

All the breath in my lungs vanished in one swift moment. Perfectly timed with Kali placing her soft hand on my bicep.

"Tell me."

Tiny creases in her brows deepened. Tightened.

"Hang tight, Levi. I'll call you back after I've spoken with Kal." Without waiting for Levi to reply, I ended the call and tossed the cell on the bed.

I peered down at her hand on my arm. Before I deciphered what it meant, how it made me feel things I'd tried to ignore, she jerked her hand back like I was on fire.

"Tell me, Brax." She crossed her arms over her chest.

How the hell did I tell her? What did I tell her?

A threat to my pack wasn't her responsibility. Hold up. Cedar Valley wasn't my pack. I gave up that birthright the second I turned my back on them and fled town like a fucking coward. I should do everyone a favor and walk out that door before I hurt someone else.

But...I'd made a vow to Zac. I promised to protect

Kali until my dying breath and so far, I'd done a shitty job of it. That ended now.

I met Kali's strong and determined gaze. "Someone..."

She waited, then became impatient and scowled at me. "Spit it out."

"Someone sprayed wolf blood all over the garage."

She didn't move or say anything. Her pale face was the only indication she even heard me. Regardless, a second later she tucked away the shock and jutted out her chin.

"We have to go back."

As much as I wanted to stay in Timber Falls avoiding every screw-up I'd ever made, I couldn't. Kali was right. The last time someone threatened my family, her brother died, and I walked away from the only life I'd ever known. No way I'd make the same mistake twice.

chapter five

Brax

I parked my truck in front of Rhett's garage, jumped out, and banged on the roller door, letting him know we'd arrived. A second later, the door rolled up and Kali drove her car into the workshop. While she transferred her things to my truck, Rhett and I ducked into the office. Neither of us bothered sitting. We wouldn't be there long.

Rhett got straight to the point. "You think the two incidents are related? A hunter? Or a rival pack?"

I'd called him earlier with the news and a plan to store Kali's car here while we returned to Cedar Valley.

So many emotions churned in my gut at the idea of returning home, but I couldn't avoid it any longer. I wouldn't let my brothers deal with a possible bloodthirsty hunter on their own. Especially one who thought it was fun to slaughter a shifter in front of our garage. Message received loud and clear. But that motherfucker better be prepared. I wouldn't slip up again.

I stuck my head around the corner to make sure Kali was out of earshot. "I dunno yet. But something tells me this latest stunt is a trap."

Not usually bothered by much, I'd never seen the guy frown—first time for everything.

"I'll send out word to the neighboring shifters. If someone's targeting Cedar Valley, we all should be on alert."

"Appreciate it." Heaviness sank on my chest, making it hard to inhale. Years before Dad died, he took me around to meet the other shifter communities. A good alpha led by example, he used to say. An even better one protected all shifters, not just his own kind. Which was how the Cedar Valley community included not only bears from time to time.

Stepping forward, I gave Rhett a brotherly hand-shake, a silent thank you and agreement between two alphas. Well, one alpha and one failed alpha. Once we ended the asshole terrorizing Cedar Valley, my screw-ups and I would head elsewhere. One of my brothers could officially become alpha and take over. I'd spent enough time here with the wolves, working under Rhett. Next, I'd head out on my own for a bit. Maybe a decade of solitude would heal my blackened soul.

Rhett clapped my shoulder while we walked out of the office into the main garage. I pulled up short. Kali had her head under a hood, checking out an engine. She raised on her toes to lean over and tinker with something, giving me a perfect view of her ass, and those beautiful legs I longed to have wrapped around my waist. Black skinny jeans or sleep shorts, it made no difference what she wore. My body reacted the same. It wouldn't let up.

Rhett cleared his throat, snapping my attention.

I almost growled at him until I caught the knowing look in his eyes. No point denying it. Kali would always be my weakness. Why the hell was fate so cruel? The sooner I dealt with this threat, the sooner I could leave again, and she could move on with her life.

The sooner she could find a worthy mate.

I ignored the sharp pain that thought created.

Rhett wandered to the front of the car and chatted with Kali while I held back at the garage entrance and got my shit together. If I started talking cars with her, the lock on those memories would burst open. Living under the protection of my family since she was fourteen, she'd spent countless weekends working on cars back home. She knew her way around an engine better than me, and that said something. She'd helped at the garage we owned in Cedar Valley, specializing in classic American muscle cars. The kind of engines that rumbled deep in my gut.

When Kali stretched up on her toes again and leaned further under the hood, pointing out something to Rhett, I dragged my eyes to the ceiling. Her bending under the hood just about sent me into cardiac arrest.

Rhett said something back, I wasn't really listening,

but the admiration in his voice confirmed everything. Team Kali had signed on another official fan. Everybody loved her. If I didn't get her the hell out of Timber Falls, Rhett might convince her to stay.

"Kal, you ready?" My voice sounded gruff. Jesus. I shoved my hands in my jeans.

She peeled herself off the car and gave Rhett a hug. His huge lumberjack build swallowed her up, and a burning sensation flashed through me. My bear stirred, a low growl building in my chest. Hang on, that was me, not my bear. Fucking hell.

Without waiting, I strode out of the garage, got back in my truck, started the engine, and cranked the heat. Kali flung open the door and jumped into the passenger side. Her soft woodsy scent slammed into my nostrils, reigniting every cell in my body. I swear I moaned. Or my bear did. Hard to tell the difference with Kali around.

"Rhett's lovely. I can understand why you'd choose to work for him."

I grunted a reply because words seemed impossible right now. All necessary brainpower diverted to the simple task of putting the truck in gear, rather than obsessing over Kali being less than an arm's length away from me. If I thought the bed was bad, this closeness was downright torture.

Backing out onto the main road, I took one final glance at Rhett's garage before skidding off down the highway. Road trip from hell coming right up.

Kali

As far as car trips went, this one was the most awkward ever. I sat there the whole time twisting my hands together in my lap, staring at the road so I didn't stare at Brax. Yet, every time I peeked out the corner of my eye, I caught him staring back, and my heart flipped. Not that I glanced often, just every minute or so to make sure he was there and not a figment of my imagination. Maybe he looked at me for the same reason.

For two years I'd thought of, okay, *fantasized*, about our reunion. In reality, it was just...weird. Some fleeting moments felt as though we'd never been apart, that I'd seen him only yesterday. That things were as comfortable and easy as they'd always been. Other times, when I caught the sorrow in his haunted expression, it felt like we were strangers. That we'd never be more.

I didn't know which hurt most.

Music didn't help. I couldn't settle on a station and in the end, turned it off. Brax didn't complain. He'd always left me in charge of the music because his playlist sucked, consisting of only three songs. Three crappy, old rock ballads. If someone found out about his sappy music choices, it would put his alpha status in serious jeopardy. Had he updated his playlist since I last saw him? Had he played those three songs on repeat for hours like I had?

I wound down the window and a rush of chilly air blew in, making me wind it back up at twice the speed. When the silence grew deafening, I finally broke. "Rhett's garage seems cool."

He grunted.

Fine. Little did he know, small talk was my specialty. *Gee, it's cold for fall, isn't it? Are you hungry? Need to stop and stretch your legs?* I could literally small talk for hours. Plus, small talk was way better than torturing myself with thoughts of what could've been or questions I didn't want answered.

Take two. "Why didn't you come home when you got the text?"

There I went. Asking a question I didn't want answered. Going by the side eyes Brax gave me, I'd hit a big fat nerve. *Ugh.* Join the club. Better he left that question unanswered. Nothing he said would heal my heart.

I twisted in the seat, angling toward the passenger door. Take three. "This part of Montana is beautiful. It reminds me of back home."

Silence. A grunt was better than complete silence. Giving up on the small talk thing, I stared at the trees passing by in a blur.

"I would've once I had answers," he mumbled.

I snapped out of my tree-gazing. "Huh?"

He didn't look at me, kept his eyes on the road ahead. "I would've called you once I knew something. I didn't want to worry you if it turned out to be a hoax or some asshole who had it out for me."

An answer. Yay him. Look at that progress.

Too bad if he didn't want to talk any further, I now did. I pivoted back to face his seat, curling one leg up under the other. "I don't understand. Why send a text after nearly two years? How could someone hold on to that knowledge for so long? What, did they wake up one day and suddenly think, oh, I better tell someone? Is it a sick hunter that likes to mentally torture their victims for years before striking again? Did they kill Zac? Is it a different hunter? Or is it a human who knows about shifters? Why text, why not just attack?"

Wow, okay. Clearly, I needed to get all those thoughts out.

A quick glance my way, then he focused back on the road. "I dunno, Kal."

The ache in my chest returned. I should try the music again. Or comment on the weather.

Brax never sugarcoated the truth. He wouldn't spin me some tale about everything being fine when it wasn't. He never lied to me. Ever. If he didn't know why we both received a text or what it meant, then that was the truth.

Right now, though, I wished he gave me more.

It must be a sick joke. It couldn't possibly be real. Why would someone murder Zac? Someone had shot him, not torn apart his body like most hunters did when they attacked shifters for their blood. Just shot him and left him there to die. Why dredge up the past now?

No one wanted answers more than me, not even Brax. If the sender knew something, I needed to find out. Until we knew more, *if* we found out more, we were all in the dark. If it turned out a hunter killed Zac, I pitied the soon-to-be-dead person responsible. No doubt Brax would gut them with his own claws and hang them in front of the garage as a warning. Shifter or not, I'd wear that blood on my hands with pride.

"Let's take one thing at a time, 'kay?"

Easier said than done.

One hand abandoned the steering wheel and reached

toward me, only to divert to the console, before returning to the wheel.

Internally, I sighed with both relief and disappointment. Being inside his truck brought back too many memories of happier times. Last night, when he brushed his fingers over my cheek, my heart all but exploded. Every cell in my body lit with a feverish flame I could never extinguish. He always affected me like that, even before he first kissed me. Ever since his dad brought Zac and I under the Archer's protection, I'd brushed off my feelings as a silly crush on my brother's best friend. I figured the infatuation would fade as we grew older. Only, it didn't. Those feelings strengthened and bloomed into something I couldn't ignore. When I found out he felt the same and we finally took a chance, my life fell apart.

Zac died. Brax left town.

Whatever lingering feelings I still harbored now didn't matter. If Brax had wanted to come home, he would have.

After two hours, Brax pulled into a gas station on the side of the highway, and I'd never been so thankful. I launched from the truck, eager for fresh air. And snacks. All that awkwardness made me hangry. I headed to the restroom first, took care of business, and splashed cool water over my parched cheeks. It didn't help me feel better on the inside, but at least I looked semi-refreshed and not a frantic mess. After, I took my sweet-ass time choosing protein bars, chocolate, and soda. Much chocolate. A girl could never have too much.

"Ready?" Brax's voice rumbled from behind me, making me startle.

Precious soda flew from the safety of my arms into the air and thumped on the floor.

"Shit!"

Brax snorted. "Jesus, Kal. Got enough food? We're going to Cedar Valley, not Australia."

I glared at him. He should know better than to stand between me and snacks. "Road trips make a girl hungry. And now the soda's all fizzy."

He scooped up the damaged bottles, and with a mischievous glint in his eyes, swapped them for fresh ones in the fridge before heading to the cashier. So evil.

I dumped my goodies on the counter beside the non-fizzy sodas.

Brax waved a hand over my takings. "All that too," he said to the cashier.

"No. I can pay my own way."

Creases deepened in his forehead, but he didn't argue. Thank God. I didn't want to have another awkward moment in front of a stranger. After paying for the gas, he waited by the door for me to finish up with the cashier.

Once back in the car and on the road, I sifted through the snack options, speaking aloud so Brax could choose his poison. "Protein bar, chocolate bar, chocolate protein bar, chocolate, crisps, more chocolate, muffin, soda, or... oh, look! A chocolate bar."

Brax laughed, a full belly laugh that I hadn't heard for so long. I missed that sound. His laugh always made me feel warm and giddy. I used to do the silliest things just to hear it. Like tickle his feet or make stupid faces at him from across the room.

I shifted in the seat so he couldn't see my cheeks flame. Flutters bloomed low in my belly, drifting down to create a sweet ache between my legs. Thankfully he couldn't spot that. Us women had it so much easier than guys. We could secretly swoon over a guy right in front of them and they'd never know.

I stilled when Brax inhaled a deep breath through his nostrils. Did he just...moan?

Surely, he couldn't smell my arousal...could he? I waited, not daring to move while I mentally processed that possibility. He couldn't...*Oh, God*. Of course, he could. His heightened sense of smell...He knew.

I sank lower in my seat, praying a hole would tear open in the car's undercarriage and swallow me.

Brax adjusted his position before clearing his throat, seeming to compose himself. Didn't matter. I was far from composed. I'd just curl up over here and drown in a pool of my own humiliation.

He held out a hand without diverting his gaze from the road. "Protein bar and non-fizzed-up soda please."

I selected his order and handed it over, taking care to avoid skin-to-skin contact.

This half of our car trip just became so much more awkward than the first half. And we still had another hour or so until we'd arrive in Cedar Valley.

Death would be less painful.

Brax ripped open the bar using his teeth, and I swallowed hard, shifting again in my seat. Probably best to watch the trees instead of fantasizing about him ripping off my clothing with those teeth. The vivid memory of that mouth devouring mine in a scorching kiss was bad enough.

I twisted the top off a soda and nearly downed the whole thing at once. But the icy fizz did nothing to simmer my overheating girl parts.

He took another bite and chewed. "Why the hell did you book into that motel?"

Right, clearly any topic was open slather now we'd been fed and watered. I didn't know what was better, his grunting non-committal responses or him engaging in the conversation. Both were potentially dangerous topics with even more dangerous answers. Either way, any topic was a distraction from the forbidden images playing on loop in my head.

I stared out the windshield and attempted a grunt of my own which came out more like a choke. Or a rabid animal's snarl.

"Kal?"

Fine. He wanted an answer, so I gave him one. "It's not like there are many options in Timber Falls. Besides, it was within my budget."

"Zac left you money."

Oh, that just pissed me off. Like I couldn't make it in this world on my own two feet. What was it with guys feeling the need to provide financially? That ship had sailed centuries ago. A twenty-five-year-old woman could make her own money, thank you very much. "The cash Zac left pays for essentials like food and bills. I bank a little from what I earn working for Harley, but it's not enough to fund extravagant search expeditions and nights in fancy hotels." I glared at him. "Especially when I didn't know how long it would take to find you or if you'd still be in Timber Falls by the time I arrived."

His fists curled around the steering wheel, knuckles going white. "I sent money—"

"You sent money back to your family." The last thing I wanted to do was fight, but Brax had no right to judge me. He left us. He left *me*. "I'm not your problem, Brax. I'm not some illegitimate child needing a monthly allowance. I'm a grown woman trying to make my own way in this world."

"That's not what I..."

How dare he expect me to accept money from him when he just upped and left me without saying a damn thing. He was hurt, well, so was I. But I didn't abandon those who needed me. I didn't abandon those I loved. I adulted and kept moving forward. Zac would've wanted that.

"Let's not fight about it, okay?" I shoved the empty soda bottle in the cup holder and pivoted to face the passenger window once again, wrapping my arms around my middle. The last thing I wanted was for him to see tears in my eyes. If I didn't look his way, I could pretend he wasn't there. "We agreed to not bring up the past. I only came so I could find the truth about Zac. After that, I'll be out of your hair."

chapter six

Brax

Heavy, dark gray clouds rolled in from the west, sending a misty wind in our direction. The late afternoon sun dipped behind the mountains. What would usually be a glorious array of colors cast over the valley now brought early darkness. Turning off the highway, I followed a dirt road through the forest, curving around the base of the mountain ranges. Kali straightened in her seat when the estate came into view in the distance. Nestled on nearly two thousand acres, the Archer Ranch had been in my family for generations. A majestic sight. Close enough to the mountains and Yellowstone River for the bears to roam, yet only twenty miles from civilization.

At the end of the drive, I parked the truck to the rear of the house and killed the engine. I sat there for a minute before turning to Kali. "I don't want this to be...weird between us."

"Me either."

I sensed she wanted to say more but held back. To be honest, so did I. Whether I wanted things to be weird was irrelevant. They still would be. When Dad took them both in just after Zac's first shift, they had no idea the shifter world existed, even though one of their parents was one. Kali had now been a part of my life for over ten years. The house contained so many memories of us that I barely remembered existing there before she arrived.

Weird didn't scratch the surface of how it would feel staying here again. Especially after everything that had happened since.

Kali opened the door, making me jolt back to the present. Deep breath. I could do this. If only my pulse stopped freaking out.

Finding answers about Zac's death was the priority. I'd push aside the nostalgia for however long it took. Which shouldn't be long, a week maximum. First thing tomorrow I'd track down the asshole that thought spraying my family's garage in shifter blood was a fun idea.

I hopped out of the truck, grabbed our bags, and followed Kali to the back door. A few feet away, the door burst open, and Levi barreled out. He lifted Kali off the ground and spun her around in a giant bear hug. "Kali-belly, you're back!"

Two days. She was gone two fucking days, moron.

The excitement level in Levi's voice didn't piss me off at all. Fine. It did.

Kali giggled with her arms locked by her side, preventing her escape even if she wanted to. It didn't seem like she minded.

"Levi, put me down! I can't breathe."

He laughed and lowered her feet to the ground.

"I'm happy you're home," Levi said, slinging an arm around her shoulders, leading her up the steps.

All good. I'd just stand out here like a loser.

At the top, Levi opened the door for Kali, and she walked inside. That was when he finally acknowledged me.

"Hey, brother."

No streamers or excited voice. All I got was a chin tip. My youngest brother stood at the top of the steps staring at me as though trying to decipher a complex puzzle.

He'd tied his dark blond, wavy hair back from his face, but strands still fell loose. He resembled an older, more mature version of the youngest Archer. Time was a bitch. While I'd been gone, everyone around me grew and aged. Why I thought time would stand still, I didn't know. Sure, I'd felt changes in myself. That was different. With Kali and Levi, I *saw* it.

I returned the chin tip. "Hey."

Kali and I could agree to no awkwardness between us

while I stayed here. It would take a hell of a lot more effort for the same outcome with my brothers.

The crease in Levi's brows deepened before smoothing out. "I'm glad you're home, Brax."

A giant lump swelled in my throat and I tried clearing it. "I'm just here until we find out who the hell sent the text. And why someone's targeting us."

Up soared the awkwardness. Levi's expression shut down fast and tight. "Whatever you say," he said over his shoulder, heading inside the house.

Awesome. Fucking awesome.

Inside was even weirder than out on the back steps. Everywhere I glanced held memories of Dad, my brothers, Zac, and Kali. Staying here was a dumbass idea. The ache in my chest awakened and expanded. I should stay in the cabin on the far side of the property. But with the threat of a potential hunter looming over our heads, I wanted Kali close. Staying in the cabin alone with her was out of the question. I couldn't control my hands last night. I'd have no hope in a secluded log cabin.

For now, staying in the house was the sensible option.

Instead of heading to my old room, I veered around the bottom of the stairs to the guest room and dumped my bag. No emotional attachments in a guest room, nor were there memories in every corner. I unzipped my bag and changed into a clean shirt. Despite it being fifty degrees outside, sweat glided down my back like a summer heatwave just hit.

Voices traveled from the direction of the living room. My timing was epic. Harley was home, too.

With Kali's bag in hand, I took the stairs to the

second floor, giving me a few more minutes to avoid the happy family reunion happening downstairs. At the end of the hall, I swung right into Kali's room but pulled up short just inside the doorway. The room wasn't how I remembered. Instead of bedroom furniture, it now contained a desk and couch. I backed out and double-checked I had the right room. *Yep.*

I dropped her bag and headed back downstairs, following Kali's voice into the kitchen. She leaned against the counter chatting with Harley, who had his head in the fridge.

"Did you switch rooms, Kal?"

Kali blanched. Her gaze shot to Harley, who straightened as he closed the fridge door.

"Welcome home, Brax."

Time also marked its changes on the middle Archer son. He'd always been the scruffy one out of the three of us, his dark red hair even darker through his full beard. He'd gotten that coloring from Mom's side. Given his ginormous shoulders, Harley still lifted truck-sized weights in the form of tires or tree trunks. The guy reminded me of Rhett, similar build and temperament. That had nothing to do with why I'd settled in Timber Falls.

Acknowledging Harley with a chin tip, I ripped off my cap. How hot did they have the thermostat? We lived in Montana, not Alaska.

"Kal? Where are all your things?"

Harley's lips tightened in a grimace. He stepped slightly in front of Kali, in a protective maneuver. Protecting her from what? Me? Why the hell would she need protecting from me? Hang on. One thought morphed into another, and all reason and common sense shot out the window. If my brother...No, surely not. He wouldn't. Would he? I glanced between them, my jaw locking tight. If Harley hooked up with Kali, I wouldn't hold myself responsible for my actions. Including another death on my bloodied hands.

My bear caught on damn quick, pacing back and forth in my head, snarling to break free. Tremors rippled through me. I fought for control. My bear wanted part of the action, but this was my fight. "Kali? Which bedroom are you sleeping in?"

"She's moved into my—"

The room spun. Colors and faces blurred together, making me dizzy. My insides twisted. Bones crunched. White-hot pain flashed through my veins as darkness took over.

***

Kali

"Kali, back up, get the hell out of the way," Harley demanded, ripping off his shirt.

"Don't." I pushed him aside. "If you shift, he'll sense a threat and tear you apart."

I hoped Brax listened to me because if he didn't, we were all in serious trouble. In front of us, his large adult-sized grizzly bared his teeth at Harley. He stalked forward, flinging a chair across the room. It smashed against the wall with a thud, shattering to pieces.

It still amazed me how Brax shifted into such a magnificent and majestic creature. But now wasn't the time to admire, not with his bear's ferocious gaze locked firmly on Harley with the intent to kill.

Grizzly bears weren't normally territorial or possessive creatures. Bear shifters on the other hand totally were.

Palm facing up, I held out my hand to his bear, slowly side-stepping away from Harley and toward the front door. Levi waltzed through the doorway between the kitchen and living room.

"Don't move," Harley snapped.

Levi froze.

"Brax?" At my voice, his bear whimpered.

I never understood how his bear responded to my voice. I thought only mates recognized their other half's voice in animal form. Perhaps because Brax had known me for years, his bear sensed I wasn't a threat. Though that didn't explain why it now targeted Harley. Regardless, I ran with that logic and side-stepped closer to the door.

His bear diverted his attention from Harley to me. "Come outside where there's more room. It's nicer out there. Cooler."

I backed to the door. Ever so slowly, I swung it open. By now, the sun had set, dropping the temperature. My coat still hung in the living room where I'd dumped it earlier. Damn it. I'd have to suffer without it. Now wasn't the time to whine about being cold or dash back inside to get it.

Harley moved. Brax's head snapped in Harley's

direction. A loud growl vibrated deep in his bear's belly. Knowing Brax was somewhere in there didn't stop my pulse from shooting through the roof. A bear was still a bear. And right now, said big freaking bear stood on his hind legs, head almost reaching the ceiling.

"Brax?" I cooed.

He turned back to me and lowered on all fours.

"Let's go outside." One slow step at a time, I backed out the door and onto the porch. Brax followed. Once down the steps and onto the lawn, he lifted his nose in the air and huffed a few cloudy breaths.

Stepping closer, I held out my hand. He sniffed my palm and whined. The sound sliced through my heart.

"Hey, big boy."

My entire body relaxed the moment his bear nuzzled into my touch. I hadn't realized how much I missed him until now, Brax and his bear. My chest squeezed so tight I couldn't breathe. How the hell could I go back to existing without him?

After another nuzzle, he turned his head to the woods. Just as well. I needed a minute or twenty to compose myself. I ruffled a hand through his bristly, rough, almost black fur.

"Go on. Walk it off. I'll be here when you're ready to come back."

Not the first time I'd said those words.

With another huff, he turned away and wandered to the woods. He peered back at me before ducking out of sight between the trees.

A few moments later, boots crunched along the

gravel path before Harley appeared at my side and draped my jacket over my shoulders.

"He always listens to you."

I walked back to the porch with him and sank down on the top step. "I just hope he comes back this time."

chapter seven

Brax

I came to on all fours, buck naked in the middle of the woods. Dirt and leaf litter stuck to my hands and knees. Cool night air exploded goosebumps along my bare skin. No idea when my bear took over or how long I'd been out here, but at some point, it rained. Wet hair clung to my forehead and shivers racked my body.

Peeling myself off the ground, I wrapped my arms around my middle and jogged toward the porch light in the distance. By a pine tree at the edge of the woods was a dry pair of jeans and a shirt. Someone must've stashed them there after the rain stopped. I tugged on the clothing, but it didn't ease the chill in my bones. I needed a hot shower.

I darted across the lawn but slowed the hell down when I spotted Kali sitting on the top step of the porch. She'd wrapped herself in a chunky knitted blanket. The one my mother made for her. She was a goddamn vision. Golden hair tumbled over one shoulder while the warm porch light swirled between a thin layer of fog, creating a glowing halo around her body. She cradled a mug between her hands, lifting it to her lips. When her eyes found mine, I swear my heart skipped a beat. Scrap that. The damn thing flat-lined. A smile ghosted across her face, yet her eyes remained guarded like she didn't know how to react or what the hell to say. That made two of us.

I paused at the bottom step, the lump once again back in my throat.

"Hey," Kali said, placing her mug on the step beside her.

She grabbed a nearby towel and tossed it to me.

"Thanks."

I attacked my hair first so icy drops stopped sliding down my back. Probably should cut it. Next, I dried my arms and the back of my neck. "How long was I out there?"

"A few hours."

Usually, my bear didn't need that long. An hour at most to run free and do bear shit. Something must've seriously pissed it off. I blinked as the events leading up to my shift resurfaced in my memory. Harley. Kali. The thought of them together had awoken both our protective instincts. Rightly so. If my bear wasn't so exhausted, he would've reared his ugly head again just to prove a point. Instead, the grizzly left me to deal with the fallout. To deal with hearing the truth. Knowing I had no right to protest their union didn't make it any easier.

Kali tucked the blanket tighter around her shoulders.

"Go inside, Kal. It's freezing out here."

She shook her head. "I need to talk to you first. Without your brothers in earshot."

That big-ass knot in my throat dropped like lead into the pit of my stomach. I didn't want to know. I couldn't hear it. Of course, I didn't expect Kali to sit around waiting for me to come home or to never move on. She deserved to find someone worthy of her love. But my fated mate hooking up with my fucking brother?

No one could blame me for losing my shit over that.

Kali patted the space beside her. I was too numb to resist, so sank down on the step.

Silence stretched between us as memories burrowed through the holes in that damn cage. Sitting on the porch step was our thing. Over the years, we'd created so many moments on these steps. But now, instead of bringing happiness, they burned like a hot iron straight through my heart.

Kali exhaled a long, drawn out breath. She stared at something on the bottom step.

"I'm not with Harley."

At least it was all out in the open. Hang on. "Huh?"

"I'm not with Harley, despite what you think. I wouldn't do that. Ever. No matter how angry I was with you after you left. He and Levi are like brothers to me, Brax. That's all. And that's all they'll ever be."

That lump lifted to somewhere midway. Relief never felt so sweet.

Kali chuckled softly. "I thought your bear was about to claw the poor guy to pieces."

"I think he was." I'd never felt that level of rage aimed at one of my brothers. I guess, when it involved a mate, we all did crazy things. "Where are all your things?"

She pivoted my way and shrugged the blanket up further. Her lips rolled inwards, her shoulders lifted and fell with a deep inhale. "After you left, I...moved into town. I rent the apartment Harley owns."

Not ideal but better than her sleeping in Harley's goddamn bedroom. "Why did you move out of the house?"

"I couldn't stay here anymore. The memories of Zac."

She peered back at the bottom step, blinking a few times.

"Of...you."

My dumbass hand ached to touch her again. To comfort her. To tell her how sorry I was. Instead, I gripped the edge of the towel. Not the same, though a much safer option.

She left this house for the same reason I did, only the memories of this place didn't haunt me more than my failures. "Kal..."

"Just because you left it doesn't mean everyone here magically stopped hurting. We didn't. I didn't."

Her words lacked bitterness, but the pain in my chest sharpened regardless. "I know."

"I just want you to know that having you back isn't easy for any of us. Especially me."

We sat there in silence for the longest moment. With the earlier rain now gone, the clouds parted revealing a scattering of glittery, bright stars. The kind that always reminded me that we were one speck in the entire universe. Only now, those stars widened the gaping hole inside my chest, putting even more distance between Kali and I despite the fact we sat side by side.

Change of topic. I gave her a sideways glance. "How many times did we sit on these steps and stargaze?"

"So many. It kinda became our thing."

She leaned her head back and stared at the sky as a soft smile curled on her mouth. Was she thinking of the same memory? The first time I kissed her was on these steps. One drizzly night, Kali had curled up beside me with a blanket wrapped around herself just like she did now. She'd laughed at something I'd said then peered up at me, mere inches from my face. In that moment everything changed. As though fate moved the planets, stilled time, and aligned all those glittery stars in one single moment. As everything in my life fell into place, so did my feelings for her. Almost like in that pivotal moment, I saw her as my fated mate, not Zac's little sister or a girl I crushed on. I saw a life with her. Overtaken with the feelings, I'd leaned in and she'd met me halfway. I'd never forget the sensation of her warm lips on mine, the sweetness of hot cocoa in her mouth, the lightning bolt that shot through my body and exploded deep in my soul.

Mentioning that was a big fat bad idea and broke the rule to not bring up the past. A rule I'd set. Besides, it would ruin this moment. Just thinking of it hurt enough.

No longer cold, I draped my arms atop my knees and

turned my attention to the stars, enjoying the first moment of peace I'd felt in a long time.

"The others are inside, waiting for you."

So much for peace. I should go inside and apologize to my brother, get that conversation over with. But I didn't want to move. For a little while longer, I wanted to sit here on the porch with Kali beside me and pretend everything was as it should be. To imagine what it would've been like if my negligence didn't result in her brother's death.

My own brother wrecked that idea. The front door opened behind us and I glared over my shoulder.

Harley stood in the threshold. "You done?"

With the blanket still wrapped around her, Kali collected her mug and stood. "Yep."

I wasn't. "Give me another minute, yeah?"

Harley tipped his chin before closing the door again.

I stood on the second step, so Kali and I were eye level. "I'm sorry 'bout earlier. With my bear. I overreacted, and I had no right. He's...*we've* always felt protective of you." That damn hand reached out and brushed my knuckles along her jaw. This time Kali turned away from my touch.

"Don't," she whispered.

The pain in her voice dropped my hand so fucking fast. She needed more from me, more than I could give. I wanted to promise her I'd stay, that I'd be here forever, and we'd live happily ever after. But the words choked in my throat. I never made promises I couldn't keep. I didn't belong here. I'd failed everyone under this goddamn roof, including her, and eventually they'd all remember.

Kali

Stupid, stupid head. Why did it have to be so damn logical? For one night, why couldn't my brain take a backseat and let my body do whatever the hell it wanted? Which, in this moment, was Brax freaking Archer.

Standing before me, he was the god of rugged sex appeal, and my body responded oh so nicely. Internally combusted was the best description. His eyes held the darkest shade of brown, bordering on black. His equally dark hair was all damp and messy, with longer strands falling over his forehead. When he wore his baseball cap, his hotness soared off the charts, but occasionally I liked him without it. Mainly so I could fantasize about curling my fingers in the thick strands while he devoured my mouth.

Soft light from the porch brought his full sleeve of ink to life. I could stare at his arms all day long. Fiery dragons, roaming bears, woodland, and something resembling the fires in hell all swirled together in a brilliant artistic masterpiece. A few newer tattoos had made it onto his arms since I'd seen him last. His dad's name and roman numerals which, if my memory served me correctly, represented the date his dad died.

I forced my shaky legs onto the top step, closer to the door. Throbbing between my legs roared to life, begging me to change my mind, to overrule my head. Just once. It would be so easy to give in, to fall back under his spell.

Brax was my first crush, my first love, and then my first heartbreak.

This time, my head was right. Damn logical brain. I couldn't do this. If I gave myself to Brax and he left again, which he'd made it clear he intended to, my heart would break in half. No, quarters. Only half remained beating from the last time he left. Could I even survive with only a quarter of a heart? Probably not.

I took another small step toward the door, away from Brax, away from his hotness, away from the overwhelming need for him to touch me. With each step, more tiny creases deepened in his forehead, and the more those muscles in his jaw worked overtime.

"Kal..." His Adam's apple bobbed.

"You really should speak to your brothers." My girl parts whined. Now wasn't the time to swoon over Brax's tall, naturally muscular physique or those smoldering dark eyes.

With a last, slightly lingering glance, I spun and walked back into the house with my head held high. Mental high five. An orgasm at the hands of Brax Archer would be so much better, but that wasn't on the menu tonight. Nor any other night.

At the hall table, I grabbed for my keys. "Shit." I'd given them to Rhett when I left my car in Timber Falls. Damn it.

"What's wrong?" Brax asked from right behind me.

I turned to face him. His truck would do. I'd walk to town if it wasn't so far, anything to clear my head. "Can I borrow your truck? I really should go home."

The angry lines deepened. A whole pack of them now sprouted over his forehead. "It's late, Kal."

"I know, which is why I want to go home. I feel like I haven't slept in years." Not an exaggeration.

"I don't like the idea of you driving back into town at this time of the night. Nor is it safe for you to be alone. You're not a shifter, but you're sure as hell connected to this pack. If it's a hunter, you're as much of a target as us. We've already talked about this."

Asshat. The man didn't even consider that I lived with someone who might be waiting for me. Possibly a big, tough growly shifter. Not a bear. Any animal but a bear.

Fine. I didn't, but that was beside the point.

Again, my stupid brain took over. Staying with the Archer brothers was safer, especially with someone targeting the family. The road into town was long, winding, and downright spooky at night. One night here wouldn't hurt. I'd done it plenty of times after I moved out, particularly on the weekends when Brax's mom organized afternoon barbeques and invited neighboring shifters.

His expression smoothed out, softened. "Please don't leave. Stay."

A crack splintered in my heart. I couldn't say no. The word wouldn't even form on my lips.

One night. In the morning, I'd borrow a truck from the garage until I got my car back. "All right."

"You can have my old room." A sinful smirk curled on Brax's lip, flashing a sexy dimple. "Unless you wanna join me in the guest room."

No way in hell. Seeing him and having him near me was bad enough. God, now I had to sleep in his old freaking bed. Which I may have done after he left, but again, beside the point. That option was better than sharing a room with him. Last night was torture. If I attempted a repeat, the ache between my legs would set the entire house on fire. "I'll take your room."

He tipped his chin again, something the Archer brothers did every time they didn't want to speak. It substituted for yes, no, go on, wait, hi, and everything in between. A whole language on its own.

Instead of responding, I trudged up the stairs. Already, I dreaded the thoughts my mind would create tonight after spending an entire day confined in a car with Brax followed by falling asleep surrounded by his things. I wouldn't sleep a wink.

chapter eight

Brax

I cracked another three eggs in the pan, watching them sizzle and bubble around the edges from the heat. On the other side of the kitchen, Harley made good work with the coffeemaker, a mandatory accompaniment for any breakfast. Any meal for that matter.

When the clear goo around the yoke turned solid white, I flipped them over. "When's Mom coming home?" I said to Harley while peering out the window. I'd never get sick of this view. Lush pines, shadowy forests, and mountains looming in the distance.

The coffee machine gurgled to life.

"I think she likes it there. I mean, she's with Aunty May and last I heard, they're taking over the town with their book club. She said she'd come home for thanksgiving."

After Kali went to bed last night, I grew some balls and chatted with Harley and Levi. No point avoiding it. They updated me on things including the garage business, what they knew about the other shifters passing through Cedar Valley, and changes in the surrounding packs. And lastly, that Mom had left to stay with her sister up in Canada for a while. Living in this house without Dad was hell for her, especially after she'd lost Zac eighteen months later.

I piled the cooked eggs onto a plate and slid them in the oven to keep warm. A new batch made it into the pan. "Probably best if she stays there until whatever this is blows over."

Harley slid a mug of steamy caffeine on the counter beside me. "Agreed."

"Good morning, losers." Levi bounced into the room, way too hyperactive for this time of the morning. For any time. The guy probably slept with a caffeine drip.

I cradled my coffee and took a long sip. One wouldn't be enough today.

Levi opened the fridge, grabbed a juice container, and chugged straight from the carton.

"The fuck, Levi?" I snapped. "This isn't some frat house. Have some fucking respect."

The little shit smirked, then padded to the cupboard and grabbed a glass.

Harley snorted. "Brax is home."

I flipped the next lot of eggs. "It's just common courtesy. I don't even want to know where that mouth has been."

Warmth bloomed at my nape a few seconds before Kali walked into the kitchen. I didn't turn around, just kept staring at the eggs, making sure they didn't burn. A different kind of heat fired through my veins, charging my blood a billion times more than the coffee ever could.

"Morning," Kali said, far more sedate than Levi.

"Coffee?" Harley asked.

"Harley, the answer is always yes. You don't even need to ask." She chuckled.

That's my girl. No, wait. She wasn't my girl. What I meant was...never mind.

The machine started gurgling again.

"Need any help?" Kali leaned her hip against the counter beside me.

I wanted to ask her how she'd slept. Was she warm enough, comfortable? Unlike me, did she get any sleep? But I couldn't. Asking her about anything related to sleeping in my room felt weird. Really weird.

"Nah, I got it. Why don't you grab a plate? These two here are yours."

Kali reached up on her toes and grabbed a plate from the top cupboard. I tried so hard not to watch her, but when her sweater lifted, I zeroed in on the hint of creamy skin at her waist. Now, not just my arm, but my whole damn body betrayed me. It took every ounce of willpower to keep my hands on the pan and spatula.

My eyes though, went totally rogue. They slid up along her sweater, all the way to the sensitive spot on her neck, then further up to her pouty bottom lip. The one I wanted to nibble on right this second.

Back on her heels, she pivoted and caught my stare. Her lips parted. She looked up at me through her long, thick lashes, and it threw me back to the moment of our first kiss, where the universe stilled, my next breath dependent on her lips touching mine. I inched closer, then remembered our company in the kitchen. That snapped my focus back to the eggs but did nothing to dampen the need pulsing through my blood. Thank fuck I stood facing the stove.

Kali held out a plate. On went her eggs, the yoke still gooey just the way she liked it. I turned off the gas and took the bacon, eggs, and hash browns from the oven, and transferred them to the kitchen table.

At the end of the table I stilled, deciding where to sit. We had this weird, silent seating chart in the family where everyone sat in the same chair at mealtimes. Creatures of habit or just because we liked the feel of a certain chair, I didn't know. But this morning, I couldn't sit where I used to.

Before Levi and Harley knew what hit them, I rounded the table and sat across from Kali, in Levi's usual chair, and piled food on my plate. Sitting here was safer than sitting beside her. Or so I thought. Changing seats threw the world off its axis. Levi diverted to where Harley usually sat, which left the big guy confused as hell and sitting at the head of the table in Mom's chair. The seat beside me, previously Zac's, remained vacant.

So much fucking chaos too early in the morning.

"If I'm staying for a bit, I need to grab some things

from my place," Kali said, sliding toast through the deep yellow yolk oozing over her plate.

Harley and Levi remained silent. Guess that was my cue to answer.

I swallowed a mouthful of bacon. "I'll take you. I wanna chat with others in town, see if they've heard anything."

The Archers were the only bear shifter pack in Cedar Valley, but the town also included a few other shifters who kept to themselves, and a handful of trusted humans who knew of our world.

"I spoke to a neighboring pack yesterday," Harley said, clearly now capable of talking. "No one's reported a missing shifter."

One good thing. "Then which pack were they from?"

"Could be a rogue. Regardless, the other packs have all offered support if we need it. No one wants another attack like what happened in Woodland Falls."

I gave a curt nod as a sharp piece of bacon jammed in my throat. The other packs probably offered their support out of respect for Dad. I hadn't exactly done anything to earn their loyalty. In the short time I was alpha, I'd let someone murder a pack member, I'd abandoned my mate, and cut myself off from my family.

Some shit alpha qualities I had.

Using the tip of the knife, I pushed around the remaining bacon on my plate, no longer hungry.

The rest of breakfast was uneventful despite the awkward seating arrangement. In fact, the banter felt like the same as before I left. More accurately, before Zac died.

Afterward, we left Levi with the dishes—served him right for drinking straight from the carton—and Kali and I headed into town. Harley drove separately to the garage to catch up on work. Another reminder of how my brothers continued to hold the fort without me. Part of me wanted to spend the day hanging out with Harley. I'd give anything to lock myself in the garage, music blaring, my head beneath the hood, forgetting all my failures. But it wouldn't matter. They'd only wait by the door until I finished. Locking those screw-ups in a box and pretending they didn't exist wasn't the solution. Believe me. I'd tried for two fucking years.

About time I faced them instead.

Kali lived in a small apartment complex with not enough security. Not even a door buzzer. Why did Harley let her stay here?

"Jesus, Kal. Anyone could just walk in."

She waved a hand, dismissing my concern. "Nothing ever happens in this town." Her breath hitched. "Well, except...besides, at some point I had to move out on my own. Your brothers tend to crowd a girl. It's bad enough staying in an apartment owned by one of them, staying in the house with all their hovering? No thanks. It drove me crazy."

At that comment, my bear and I stirred in unison. Harley and Levi crowding Kali was better than some asshole taking advantage of her. She was my mate for fuck's sake. Which, of course, she still didn't know.

Kali unlocked the door, swung it open, and I followed her in. At least the inside was in better shape.

"I'll just be a minute," she said, veering off to what I assumed was her bedroom.

I halted in the living room, searching for signs of another guy living here. She hadn't mentioned one, I just needed to confirm that shit for myself. Put it down to the imaginary claim I had on her. Stupid, I know. I lost any right to claim her as mine after I left. My bear clearly ignored the memo though and still burned a candle for her, patiently waiting for the day we'd reunite. A mate destined by fate wasn't easy to get over.

By the couch, a small wooden picture frame drew me closer. A selfie of Kali and me that she'd taken at some festival we'd attended. I couldn't remember the occasion or the year, but she was maybe sixteen? What I did remember was how the summer sunshine glimmered on her skin. The way her laugh ignited a spark deep within my soul. How, with just one look, my heart beat a little faster.

Back then she didn't know I loved her. Hell, I doubt I realized either. We were just two friends hanging out. I didn't understand our connection, let alone acknowledge it, even though those feelings had simmered in the background from the moment I first met her, growing, and intensifying over the years. In that picture, we both looked so happy, so carefree. As though our lives were ours to live and nothing would stand in our way.

Why was fate so cruel? Now instead of happiness, the memory caused a wicked pang behind my ribs.

I needed to leave. I couldn't surround myself with these memories a minute longer. Facing my screw-ups was one thing. Acknowledging how much I ached for a life with Kali? A whole other level.

I stalked to the bedroom and found Kali humming to herself, folding each item of clothing in a meticulous manner before placing it neatly in an overnight bag on the bed.

"Hey, you almost done?"

She paused, black lacy panties dangling in her hand. I didn't look. Much. Why couldn't she hold a chunky sweater? Jesus.

"Yeah. Why? What's wrong?"

I swallowed, dragging my gaze from the scrap of fabric. "Nothing. I'm just..." *Sorry. Heartbroken. Lost without you.* "Hungry."

So pathetic.

Her suspicious gaze narrowed a second before she tossed the panties in the overnight bag and padded to me, stopping just out of reach. "Brax?"

Now wasn't the time to sift through my new revelations. I wasn't even sure I wanted to air them. Would it change anything? Probably not. Telling Kali how much I missed her wouldn't bring her brother back.

Her gaze slid to the picture frame I still cradled in my hand like a lifeline. A warm smile lit her eyes.

I offered it to her. "You wanna pack this?"

That smiled faded. "No bringing up the past, remember?"

The words left a bitter taste in my mouth. Served me right for thinking that rule would work. Everywhere I looked reminded me of our past. Every smell, every taste, every goddamn song reminded me of her. A picture of happier times only contributed to the overflowing list.

I hated that I'd hurt her. Even more so, I hated how all that pain still lingered between us.

I gently tossed the frame on the bed and tugged Kali into my arms, holding her tight. Her body stiffened for a second before relaxing into my big, beary hug. Being a bear shifter came with advantages. With her cheek pressed against my thumping heart, I rested my chin atop her head and inhaled a deep breath of warm sunshine. So fucking good. Her arms snaked around my lower back, gripping my shirt, clutching me as tightly as I held her.

Peace. Right here, right now, my soul found peace.

We stayed, safe and secure in each other's arms for ages, lost in our own ideal world where none of the bad shit between us ever happened.

Our height difference was perfect. Enough for me to cocoon her in my embrace, but not too much I needed to crouch to kiss her. Not that I'd kissed her while standing. The first and only time I kissed her had been when we sat side by side on the porch steps.

Now images of her soft lips flooded my mind. I imagined taking her mouth with mine, crushing her body against me, her fingers raking through my hair. For a heartbeat, I wanted it all. I wanted to fall asleep with her beside me. I wanted to wake each morning with her naked body draped over mine, her long golden hair splayed out over my chest. I wanted to worship her with my tongue until she writhed with need beneath me. Most of all, I wanted to kiss her again. The urge so great a low growl rumbled in my chest.

Man, I needed to get my shit together and focus. How could I crave any of that? Especially now.

I loosened my hold and took half a step back.

Mood now broken, Kali slipped her hands around my sides to place them flat on my chest, one over my heart.

I peered down into her bright hazel eyes. "How 'bout we grab some burgers while we're in town?"

Another nostalgic trip down memory lane couldn't hurt. *Yeah right, dumbass.*

Her smile returned, and I swear my heart had never felt so whole.

"I'd love that. I'll finish packing."

I nodded, forcing my arms back by my side, reluctant to let her go even though we were still in the same room. Stupid. I'd let her go once before. Though now I knew what that felt like, I wasn't sure I could ever do it again.

On her way to the bathroom, Kali grabbed the picture frame and slipped it into her overnight bag. Warmth swelled inside my chest. Our past was complicated and full of way more pain than anyone should endure. But it also consisted of moments like those in the photo. Moments that bought us joy and reminded us of the simple things in life we often took for granted.

It reminded me of us.

I couldn't ignore my past any longer, and to be honest, that tactic never truly worked. My past connected me to Kali. It always would.

And I'd never forget that again.

chapter nine

Kali

After chatting with a few locals about the murdered wolf at the garage, Brax drove us to the main street of town where we grabbed burgers and milkshakes from Rob's Café. The guy made the best burgers in the county. Probably in the entire state of Montana. Instead of eating there, we drove to the lookout on the Archer property and sat in the bed of Brax's truck overlooking Cedar Valley. Our burgers were probably cold by now, but it didn't matter. Nothing topped this view.

Despite the clear day, the brisk wind and shadowy trees chased away the sun's warmth. Brax draped a blanket over our legs and settled in beside me. Not that I needed more heat. Being this close to him was enough to make a girl combust. I'd discovered that last night. He shuffled closer until his arm brushed mine, sending my senses into overdrive.

I murmured a thanks and tore open the wrapping before taking a giant bite of my burger. Meat juice dribbled down my chin, and I giggled, slopping it up with my thumb. So graceful. At least with a mouth full of meat and carbs I wouldn't say anything stupid. Back at my place, when he'd hugged me, I swore something shifted between us. As though we'd battled an imaginary war for centuries and this morning, we both woke not knowing how or why it'd started.

When he'd wrapped his arms around me, I wanted to believe he'd changed his mind. That he'd stay. That he loved me as much as I loved him. My feelings for him had never dimmed during our time apart. If anything, they morphed into something more than physical attraction. A soul deep connection that became a part of me, always there, humming beneath the surface. Sure, him leaving sucked, but my heart never stopped aching for him to return. Hoping he would. And now he sat beside me in the bed of his truck, just like we had so many times before, and I couldn't stop myself from wanting it to be real.

Wanting *us* to be real.

Dangerous thoughts right there. So, so dangerous.

I swallowed the mouthful of burger and peered at the view. Midday sun shone on the mountain, turning the pine trees a vibrant, lush green. Snow scattered the bare patches of earth, the sun no longer warm enough to melt it. Sprawled at the foot of the mountain was the Archer ranch with the small town of Cedar Valley in the distance.

Up here, surrounded by wilderness, I'd always felt at home.

"People would kill for this view." I winced. Wrong choice of words. "I mean..."

Brax nudged my arm with his, sending tiny sparks through my blood. "I know what you meant."

He pulled a chunky pickle from his burger and held it out for me. I stared at it, pinched between his fingers, as though it were about to sprout wings and fly over the cliff. Brax always gave me his pickle. Always. It became something as normal as the sun rising each day. He could easily order a burger without, but I guess he knew how much I loved them. One pickle on a burger was never enough. Now though, the simple act of offering it to me caused that pang in my chest to steal my breath.

Did he eat the pickle when he was in Timber Falls? Did he order burgers without them?

Did he...give his pickle to someone else? Okay, that sounded weird. But still...I ached to know.

A heavy weight squeezed my ribs. He'd never mentioned seeing someone, but that didn't mean he hadn't moved on. Would he tell me if he did?

How could a stupid pickle make things so confusing?

I gave a little shake of my head. Brax frowned, probably wondering what the hell was wrong with me before he tossed the offending vegetable over the side of the truck. My stomach cursed. I'd love nothing more than to eat that pickle and pretend things were easy, but they weren't. Instead, I placed my half-eaten burger on a napkin in my lap and picked at my fries. Thanks to a damn vegetable, my mood transformed from sweet and nostalgic to painful.

"Did you miss...home?" *Me. Did you miss me?*

I couldn't stop myself from asking. I had to know.

I almost held my breath, waiting for Brax to finish chewing the last mouthful of his burger. Why did I torture myself like this?

Using a napkin, he wiped the grease off his fingers before bundling his trash into the takeout bag. He relaxed back against the truck's rear window and took a long draw of his strawberry milkshake, staring at the valley.

Had I thought it? Maybe the words never came out of my—

"After a while, I found myself doing things like this. Grabbing a greasy burger, heading to the lookout in Timber Falls, and eating it in the bed of my truck. The view wasn't half as good as here, nor was the burger, but it made me feel...I dunno, a little closer...to you."

A crack splintered in my heart. How long had I wanted him to say those exact words? But now hearing them hurt. Bad. Part of me wanted to resent him for doing things that made him feel closer to me when he could've just come home. But who was I to judge? I'd done the same.

I fiddled with a fry. "At night, I used to sit on the back steps and peer at the stars, wondering if you were doing the same."

Brax exhaled a ragged breath and slid his gaze to me. "I was. Every fucking night."

My heart exploded. I almost wished he hadn't replied. That would've been easier.

Brax reached over and curled his fingers in mine. His thumb drew a lazy circle over the top of my hand, making butterflies burst from a cage low in my belly. Why did this feel so right?

Fries forgotten, I shuffled closer and rested my cheek on his shoulder, feeling more content and protected than I had in years. As teenagers, Brax always picked me up from school every Friday and we'd spend the afternoon here stuffing our faces with burgers and milkshakes. I'd tell him about my day, exam results, plans for the weekend, friend drama. He'd sit and listen, offering encouragement or advice at all the right moments.

What advice would he offer me now? Would he tell me to bare my soul and ask him to stay? Or would he tell me to move on with my life, that I was better off without him?

Probably the latter. Only problem, it didn't matter what he said. I believed he was worth it. He was the only one for me.

We only had one shot at this life. What if he was mine?

Curled up on the couch in front of the fire, Brax's mom used to tell me stories of fated mates, how each shifter was born with only half a soul and spent their entire life searching for their other half. How they were never truly whole until they found their mate. Brax's parents had found each other when they were kids. The strength in their bond evident by how they'd loved each other so fiercely. When Brax's dad passed away, a piece of his mom died with him.

I'd never considered myself Brax's mate. Wouldn't the other half of his soul be a shifter? That made more sense than him having an ordinary human mate like me. But in moments like this, a spark of hope clawed its way into my heart. What if I was his mate? What if the universe destined us to be together? What if that was why I felt so connected to him?

I opened my mouth to say something, not quite sure what, but Brax's cell rang. Without letting go of my hand, he placed his milkshake down and grabbed it. Harley's name flashed on the screen.

Brax lifted the cell to his ear. "Yeah."

I straightened and crossed my legs, pivoting slightly to face him. He tightened the hold on my hand as though I was about to leave. I wasn't. Nothing had ever been clearer.

"Hang on." He lowered the phone to hold it between us. "Kali's here, too. You're on speaker."

Harley's voice came through the handset. "Bad news."

"What is it?" I asked.

"I just saw...Jack Preston."

The truck bed fell out from beneath me.

"Fuck," Brax growled. "Are you sure?"

Black flashed in his pupils as his bear raged, preparing to shift and those muscles in his jaw tightened like crazy.

"Damn sure. I was leaving the store when I saw him drive past. Brax, if he's back in town..."

Harley didn't need to finish that sentence. We all knew what it meant.

Dots connected. A whole line of them. Shit, shit, shit. The text, the dead shifter at the garage, and now my father appearing in town. Coincidences didn't exist in this world.

I opened my mouth to speak, but Brax beat me to it. "Meet us back at the ranch."

"Got it."

Brax ended the call. He let go of my hand to send a quick text, followed by another. I presumed he raised the alarm. Just as well. With Jack Preston in town, the more people who knew, the better.

Like a man on a mission, he bundled up the blanket and our trash while I sat there stunned, trying to process the latest development. My father? Here in Cedar Valley?

Brax leaped over the side of the truck in a move that would heat my panties under better circumstances. Turning back to me, he gripped my hips and lifted me out of the bed, not letting go even when my feet touched the ground.

Seconds ago, I had my head on his shoulder, dreaming about a life with him. Now, that life was in danger.

"Brax."

He must've heard the quiver in my voice because his expression softened. "We gotta get back. It's not safe out here in the open like this."

"I know. I just wish we had...more time."

He pulled me in, wrapping his arms around my shoulders. "Me too, baby. More than you could ever know. But I won't let that asshole hurt you."

I shuddered at the memory of the last time I saw my father. Fourteen years old, waking with his hands squeezed around my neck. Zac had burst into my room and shifted for the first time, transforming into a freaking bear. I'd never forget the sadistic smile on my father's face the moment Zac attacked him. As though Zac had done exactly what my father intended. My father turned into a raging monster as he fought Zac, until Zac's bear over-powered him, and he'd fled.

Jack resurfaced every couple of years, spotted in neighboring towns, but never contacted me or Zac, as though we were nothing to him. Fine by me. Never knowing our mother was bad enough, but having a father who attacked his own children? We were better off without him in our lives.

I inhaled a deep breath, composing myself. Brax was right. We needed to get to the safety of the Archer ranch. I eased back out of his embrace.

He cupped my face between his hands. "I'll protect you, Kal. I promise." Layered in his voice was all the unwavering determination I wished I felt.

Leaning down, he placed a gentle kiss on my fore-head as though it sealed his vow of protection.

If only it were that simple.

chapter ten

Kali

Noise from the TV hummed in the background while some action movie played on the screen. No idea which one. Hard to concentrate when all I did was try to tune into Brax's phone conversations. That cell remained glued to his ear all afternoon as he stalked back and forth from the study. Harley returned home about an hour after Brax and me. He strode into the office with Brax and shut the door. Seven minutes later, Harley left via the back door while stripping off his shirt. His bear growled outside shortly after.

"Levi?" Brax barked from the doorway to the study.

Levi barreled down the stairs. "Yo."

I cocked my ear toward the conversation, leaning further over the side of the couch.

"Call that buddy of yours on the force, yeah? Let him know who's in town."

"Consider it done." Heavy footsteps raced back upstairs.

That told me absolutely nothing. No clues at all.

The tension in the house skyrocketed from a minor inconvenience to catastrophic in a matter of hours. Screw this. I wouldn't sit around waiting for answers, nor was I some helpless female they drip-fed information to whenever it suited them. This whole thing started with a text sent to me. Okay, me and Brax, but still. I'd found Brax. I'd convinced him to come back to Cedar Valley. He promised to keep me in the loop.

With that logic, I lasted another few seconds, four to be precise, before I tossed the blanket off my legs and marched into the study.

Poor guy had his palms braced on the desk with his head hung, deep in thought.

Too bad. I couldn't wait any longer. "Brax Archer, I've been part of this family for over ten years. I deserve to know what's going on. You promised." Throwing my hands on my hips wouldn't intimidate Brax, I knew that, but it helped with my confidence.

Brax straightened and spun to face me, leaning his butt on the desk. "A few packs spotted your dad passing through. Last night, a hunter attacked a wolf eighty miles out of town."

Wow. I nearly keeled over. He actually told me.

Naturally, I rolled with it, kept that momentum going. "It might be a coincidence."

Brax cocked his brow. Okay, I didn't believe that either.

"Yeah, but...a hunter? My father?"

If my father was a hunter, that meant my family descended from an ancient coven of witches. One who performed a blood ritual centuries ago to annihilate shifters. Only, it backfired, resulting in a bloodthirsty hunter curse passed down through generations.

His lips thinned into a tight line. "It fits. When Dad and I found you in the diner, you said that when your father attacked Zac, his eyes turned to thin amber slits."

I shuddered at the memory.

"If my father is a hunter, then my mother must've been a shifter because Zac was a bear."

How the heck did that work? How could my mother love someone who hunted her kind for their blood?

My father was crazy, but being a hunter took that crazy to the next level.

Heaviness sank low in my gut. I wasn't a shifter. Which meant... "Will I turn into...?"

Brax shook his head. "Don't even go there, Kal. You've been around shifter blood over the years and never reacted. You're not a hunter. Nor will you ever be."

How could he be so sure? What if I changed? From what I knew, a descendent needed to ingest shifter blood to activate the hunter curse. So far, I hadn't drunk any blood meals. Not that I ever wanted to. *Yuck.* I'd also never experienced any witch skills.

Great. A failed witch and shifter. More evidence I didn't belong anywhere.

I tried not to dwell on that last part for the umpteenth time. "What do we do?"

"I've called in a few favors."

The shifter community always banded together in times of crisis. And right now, was exactly that—a crisis. Thanks to living with the Archer family, I knew enough about how it operated. An alpha represented each community. Brax became Cedar Valley's alpha when his dad passed away three years ago. As the eldest Archer brother, he excelled at the position until Zac...Well, nothing like the death of one of your pack to shred your alpha confidence.

Harley stood in for Brax when he left, but the position wasn't for him. Some people were born leaders, others weren't. Brax was the former.

Pushing off the desk, Brax slid his cell into his back pocket and strode to me, lingering an arm's length away. "You're safe with me."

How could a parent be so cruel? How our father survived that night, I'd never know. I was too shocked at my brother's transformation to consider chasing him or calling the police. Before then, we'd never known shifters existed, let alone the fact my brother was one. The second Zac returned to human form, he'd packed our bags, and we fled to Cedar Valley, drawn to the neighboring town by some mysterious pull. Harry Archer found us in the diner and took us in.

I shook off the memory, focusing on the here and now. Raw possession fired in Brax's deep brown eyes sending a burning shiver down my spine. I pitied anyone who tried to hurt me. For example, my father. Brax would tear him to pieces.

The longer I lost myself in his intense gaze, the more the air charged between us. Every nerve ending sparked and tingled, sending a burst of heat through my blood. My pulse thrummed in my ears, so loud I was sure Brax could hear it.

God, I craved him more than a woman should. More than I should. Every time we found our gazes locked like this, I swore the earth fell out from beneath my feet. I wanted to fall. I wanted to dive in headfirst and never come up for air.

I just wanted him.

Last time he looked at me like this, he'd kissed me. Or maybe I'd kissed him. Hard to tell who instigated the moment that forever changed my life.

Standing here before him was another one of those pivotal moments. A fork in the road. Turn right and retreat to emotional safety, no involvement with the guy I crushed on for almost half my life. The same guy who confessed feelings for me only to leave town a few days after as though I didn't matter. Or I could choose the reckless option. Turn left and enter a world of unbelievable passion with Brax even if only for a short time. Accepting that option risked crushing my heart again.

Would the benefits outweigh the risk? My body thought so. But how about my head?

His fingers brushed my hand ever so slightly before curling his index finger around mine.

My heart pounded. Little thrills of warmth shot

through my middle, pooling between my legs. I needed to be more careful around him. With only a look, he spun my world out of control until I ached for him to lay me on that desk and have his way with me. Imagine all the wicked things he could do with those beautiful full lips. I'd only kissed them once, and that ruined kissing anyone else for the rest of my life. I wanted to repeat that moment. I needed it more than my next breath.

I glided closer. My body overruled my brain. Turned out my feet had a mind of their own.

Desire flashed through Brax's eyes. They dipped to my mouth. "Kal..."

A warning rang in his low, rough voice. This was a bad idea. To be honest, I kind of agreed. Not great timing. But I was too far gone to stop. My mouth watered for his, to taste his lips, feel his warmth pressed firmly against me.

"It's okay..." I whispered, now so close to him our breaths mingled in the sliver of space between our lips.

Ever so slowly, he let go of my hand to cup his fingers around my nape, thumb resting on my jaw stroking back and forth. He paused, giving me an out, a chance to turn right instead. An opportunity to protect myself from inevitable heartbreak. Pity I didn't want to. If kissing Brax Archer again resulted in my heart falling apart, then so be it. Kissing him for the first time on the front porch two years ago felt right. So did this. Our timing always sucked. I had to seize the moment.

As though he sensed my thoughts, he leaned down, and I rose on my toes to meet him halfway. His lips pressed against mine in the gentlest kiss I'd ever experienced. Warm, soft, and heartbreakingly beautiful. So different from our first kiss. As though memories of laughter and pain, of desire and longing, seeped into the layers of this kiss. Not simply the caressing of two mouths.

Little bolts of pleasure shot through my middle, swirling around and exploding in a wild hot mess. Determined not to make a fool of myself and climb the man like a tree, I held it together and let him lead. Restraint was the key here.

Well, that didn't last. His tongue teased along my bottom lip, urging me to open for him. Restraint was for losers anyway. I wasn't scared of a damn thing. Besides a broken heart, but I'd already decided that risk was worth it.

I opened my mouth and let restraint fly out the window. Brax got the hint. His free hand cradled the other side of my jaw, tightening his hold, angling my head. I surrendered to all the sensations, all the emotions I'd harbored inside for far too long. I reveled in the way my knees wobbled, the fiery pulses throbbing between my legs, and how he made me see stars with one freaking stroke of his tongue.

This kiss would go down in history as my best kiss. Ever. I pitied everyone across the universe who never experienced a kiss this passionate. This man's skill in the tongue department was off the charts. If that mouth ever got to other parts of my body, I'd be in a world of trouble. Or heartbreak. Again, hard to decide.

I moaned, fisting his shirt, tugging him flush against me. I needed more. I ached to touch him, strip him naked, wrap my legs around his waist while he carried me to that desk—

The memory hit me like a vicious tornado. It flattened me, crushed my soul, and destroyed everything I had. *Sitting on the porch steps...Brax trailing kisses along my neck...Zac's bear growling from deep in the woods...A gunshot...The sickening cry piercing through the night.*

My lips stilled. So did Brax's. Tears burned behind my closed lids.

He rested his forehead against mine, keeping my face firmly in his grasp. His chest heaved in and out with heavy breaths colliding between us. Violent shocks rippled through my body. My legs weakened. I sucked in gasps of air, drowning under the emotion.

"Breathe, baby," he murmured. "Just breathe."

His thumbs swept back and forth along my jaw.

I couldn't. My throat closed so tight, preventing air from entering. I wanted to step back, escape his embrace and the intimacy, but he wouldn't release me. He kept still and silent, his thumbs the only part of him moving. Gradually, the soothing strokes chipped through the tightness in my chest and spilled light and warmth into my soul, steadying my racing heart.

Brax

I never intended to kiss her. Kissing her was the last thing she needed, and really, I wasn't sure how we got to that point. I didn't want to screw things up any further.

Giving in to my feelings for her only resulted in more complications.

The universe had a sick sense of humor, and I fucking hated it.

Two years ago, I asked Zac's permission to date his little sister. The guy knew Kali and I were destined. He never said it aloud, but he knew. I'd never forget the cheeky grin on his face when he told me it was about fucking time. Then he shifted and headed out to patrol the woods for a few hours, instead of me. Code for: get your ass into gear, man.

I'd never been so goddamn nervous with a girl. But Kali wasn't just any girl. She was *my* girl. That night on the porch steps, as we gazed at the stars, I poured my heart out to her. I'd told her how I felt. How I ached for more from our friendship. How I hoped she'd give me a chance to show her how much she meant to me. She'd given me the cutest grin before leaning in and kissing me.

Instead of that night being the start of something new, something magical, it was the night my family fell apart.

The night Zac died.

I eased back a little to see Kali's face. Tears ran down her cheeks, the tip of her nose red, her lips swollen from our kiss. She blinked a few times before lifting those thick, wet lashes to look up at me. I diverted my thumbs to wipe away her tears.

"I'm sorry." Seeing her hurt like this sucker-punched me right in the gut. "I'm so fucking sorry."

She lifted her hand and placed it on my chest, over

my thumping heart. "Don't. I wanted to kiss you. It's just..."

Why the hell did it hurt so bad? "I get it."

The office door flung open. I glanced sideways at the soon-to-be-dead fucker. Levi strode in, halted, his confused gaze darted between Kali and me before he backed the hell out. "I'll, ah...wait out here," he said, closing the door.

"Talk about ruining a moment." A soft smile lifted her cheeks, but it didn't reach her eyes. "You should see what he wants. It might be urgent."

"He can wait." I breathed a heavy sigh, exhaling all the shitty emotions I struggled to deal with. "My priority is you."

Kali was, and always would be, my priority. That would never change. How I thought I could function in life without her was beyond me. Until now, I hadn't realized I'd operated in a fog, my numb ass moving one foot in front of the other for the past two years. Being back near her, touching her, inhaling her scent, gave my demons peace. Gave my heart hope.

Kali stepped back, and this time, I lowered my hands and let her go. Last thing I wanted was for her to resent me more than she already did.

"I'm okay, Brax. Really. I just got a little emotional, that's all." She glanced at the door. "I'm actually a bit tired, so I'm heading to bed."

I wanted to tell her not to leave. To ask her to stay with me. But mostly I wanted to wrap my arms around her, not only to make sure this moment was real, but to also comfort her. So much emotional baggage hung between us that I wanted to unpack, but now wasn't the time. After we took down the threat to our family, I'd sit down with her and sort out this mess. I'd get down on my knees and beg for her forgiveness. Until then, I'd keep my hands to myself.

I anchored my feet to the floor as Kali turned and walked out the door.

A few seconds later, Levi strode in, closing the door behind him. "You sure hooking up with Kali right now is a smart idea?"

I wanted to punch the little punk in the face. "For starters, I'm your fucking brother, not some loser trying to take advantage of her. And second, we weren't hooking up. We kissed." I stormed to the other side of the desk and braced my hands on the top. "Not that it's any of your business."

Levi remained by the door, arms crossed over his chest. "I don't want her getting hurt. You know, like last time."

Where was the brotherly loyalty? Imaginary daggers stabbed my chest, twisting until they left gaping holes oozing with blood. I should be thankful my brothers felt so protective of her, they always had, ever since Kali and Zac came into our lives. But now, that protectiveness just pissed me off. "Kali and I are both adults. We can make our own decisions."

"Then why won't you tell her she's your mate?"

Telling my brothers what I felt for Kali was a big fat mistake. Though, at the time, I hadn't known our future would unfold as it did.

My hands tightened on the edge of the desk, bulging my knuckles. "She deserves better."

Levi hardened his stare and for a minute, I thought he'd argue, but he didn't. Case closed.

He sank into the armchair, crossing his leg to rest an ankle on his knee. "I spoke to my buddy on the force."

Change of topic. Best idea yet. "What'd he say?"

"They're still trying to trace the text. He's swamped right now. But he said that Jack Preston is a wanted man in the shifter community for a long list of reasons. He also confirmed that they believe he's...a hunter."

"Not the most surprising news."

"Yep. He issued an arrest warrant with the human police too, so if that lowlife slips up, someone will grab him. I hope a shifter gets him first."

If only it were that easy. That asshole had been on the shifter radar ever since he tried to kill Zac. No one had caught him though. Every time he resurfaced, he vanished soon after. Shifters governed their own laws and punishments. We couldn't serve a sentence in a human jail and risk revealing our world. Threatening the life of a shifter carried a death sentence, one delivered by the pack's alpha. If it came to it, I'd do exactly that.

I gave Levi a curt nod. "Thanks, man."

"No worries."

Levi remained seated. Was he waiting for an invitation to leave?

"Something else?" I asked, with more snark in my tone than intended.

Levi's mouth scrunched up at one side. No words came out.

"Spit it out, Levi."

"Don't mess around with her unless you intend to stay, Brax. It's not cool."

The words punched the pit of my stomach. I didn't respond and didn't need to. Levi stood and strode out the door.

chapter eleven

Kali

I lay there wide awake in Brax's oversized bed for hours. Felt like years. Tossing and turning didn't lure sleep my way, neither did adding or removing clothing. Nor did tugging the blankets up. Nothing helped. Restlessness consumed my entire body. Not just because of the situation with my father and the possibility of being related to a bloodthirsty killer, but also from my kiss with Brax.

The gentle and loving way he cradled my face in his hands and made me feel all warm and safe. The yearning that soared through me when his mouth pressed against mine. What did it mean? Would he stay? Would things return to how they once were? Could we have a future? Or, when he eliminated the threat to his pack, would he leave again?

I didn't have those answers. Hence the reason my stupid brain wouldn't shut the hell up and let me sleep. Earlier, right before we kissed, I'd decided that further heartbreak was worth the risk. No risk, no reward, Levi used to joke. But now that my head had once again resumed making semi-sound decisions, was I prepared for the fallout? Could I survive another heartbreak if Brax left?

No. I'd never recover.

But maybe, just maybe, another saying was also true. Something about having loved and lost was better than not loving at all. I loved Brax with every cell in my body. I couldn't stop even if I tried. Was there any point fighting it? Denying my feelings left me in a stagnant wasteland of nothingness.

I flipped onto my back and huffed a breath. That didn't help either. Nothing would. My overthinking brain cursed me to lay here awake for eternity.

Just before midnight, the bedroom door creaked open. A shadow slipped inside the room before the door softly latched again. Thanks to my hours of wakefulness, my eyes had adjusted to the darkness enough to know the sizeable shadow belonged to Brax.

My heart, previously in a resting state, jolted to life. It pounded so fast it buzzed in my oversensitive ears.

I tracked Brax as he crossed the room to the opposite side of the bed. The mattress dipped when he lowered on top of the covers, stretching out on his back. My breath jammed in my throat. Scrap that, I stopped breathing altogether.

Brax sighed as though he missed his mattress. A pang of guilt tightened my chest. I should be downstairs in the guest bedroom, not him. This was his family home, his bedroom, not mine. I had no right to be in here.

When Brax began softly snoring, his breathing slow and steady, I relaxed a little. He wasn't here to talk nor address the big fat elephant in the room that was our kiss. He came seeking the sanctuary of his bed. I could deal with that.

As slowly as I could, so I didn't wake him, I maneuvered onto my side facing him, tucking one hand under my pillow. He'd fallen asleep fully clothed, except for his boots, with his hands resting flat on his stomach. Maybe he sleepwalked here, subconsciously drawn to his bedroom. Or he was so damn tired he didn't realize he'd wandered to this room by mistake. Either way, it didn't matter. Once my heart calmed down, having him sleep next to me soothed my soul. Again, a sense of peace and protection swelled inside me.

By the pale moonlight filtering through the uncovered window, I studied the side profile of his beautiful face. The guy was a god, even in the darkness. Strong, square jaw dusted in a short dark stubble, high cheekbones, perfect full lips. Thick coiled muscles roped his arms and up the side of his neck, making his t-shirt stretch in all the right places.

How sad that our story never truly began. What

would life be like if Zac was still alive? Would Brax and I be together? Be happy?

As though he sensed my thoughts even in his sleep, he rolled onto his side facing me. Our faces were now inches apart. His tattooed arm lay between us, and I couldn't stop myself from reaching out, sliding my hand over his. Seeking comfort or familiarity, I didn't know. I needed to touch him in some small way. Having him close made the ache in my heart more bearable. In his slumber, his fingers curled around mine.

I stared at his closed lids, praying he would open them, yearning for him to kiss me again. Only, he never woke. Probably for the best.

chapter twelve

Brax

I woke. Early, going by the soft morning light invading the room. Golden light splashed over the walls while I lay on my back staring at tiny dust particles fluttering in the air above my head. The stillness, peacefulness, a calming relief. As though my brain only dealt with one revelation at a time, the heavy weight draped across my middle registered next, followed by the warm breath exhaling on the crook of my neck. Glancing sideways, I found Kali curled up in my arm.

What the hell?

Lifting my head slightly, I scanned the room.

Familiar nightstand, dresser, and painting hung on the wall. I wasn't in the guest room. Somehow, in the middle of the night, I'd wandered to my old room by mistake. Shit. I glanced at Kali. I couldn't untangle us even if I wanted to. Which I didn't. She had her arm over my stomach, her head on my upper arm and her body so flush against mine, we may as well be one.

Things progressed from bad to worse when I noticed she'd slept in nothing but a tank top and panties. At least I had the decency to fall asleep fully clothed. My morning hard-on rocketed to a new level as my veins diverted blood like my life depended on it. Jesus. I needed to detangle myself and get the hell out of the room before she woke. If I could only slide my arm out from underneath her head.

Kali stirred, murmuring something in her sleep and her leg tucked over mine. Heat seeped through the fabric of her panties onto my thigh, making me groan. She had me locked in her grasp and although I shouldn't enjoy it, I couldn't help but relish in the sweet satisfaction. For years, I'd ached to have her legs wrapped around me. Even fully clothed, with her asleep, the moment was bittersweet. A secret memory to cherish.

With that fucked up logic, I curled my arm drawing her closer. The combined floral smell of her hair and the woodsy scent of her skin became an epic tonic. I inhaled a deep, full breath, savoring every scent and storing it in my memory.

"Did you just smell my hair?" she murmured, her voice groggy from sleep.

A silent chuckle quaked my insides. Busted. "Good morning."

She wriggled in my embrace, turning half on her stomach to peer up at me.

"Seriously, did you smell my hair?"

Her tone wasn't angry, intrigued maybe. I shrugged my free shoulder. "It always smells nice. Reminds me of home."

Her lips rolled into a tight line. "You shouldn't say things like that."

Words choked in my throat. I wanted to say sorry, that I didn't mean it, but that would be a lie. I never lied to her. Her scent, the sound of her laugh, the sparkle in her bright hazel eyes always reminded me of home. I needed that now more than ever.

She propped herself up on one elbow. Blood rushed through my arm as it exploded with pins and needles. I clenched and unclenched my hand, so the sharp sting ended quicker. When I could move my arm again, I lifted it. What I should've done was drag it out from underneath her. Instead, I tucked a strand of hair behind her ear before resting my palm on her bare shoulder.

She tilted her head, leaning into my touch, her eyes softening. On a scale of bad ideas, this was right at the top. Being in bed with Kali, that sexy just-woke-up look in her eyes, and her golden hair tumbling over one shoulder, was the most dangerous situation I'd ever encountered. If I stopped touching her, I might escape with only surface wounds.

Ha. Not likely.

I trailed a feather-light path down her back and up

again, amazed at how natural it felt waking with her in my arms. Sure, we touched over the years when we both lived in this house—wrestled for the TV remote or the last bag of popcorn kind of touching. It never bloomed into something more sexual. Physically anyway. Mentally, I'd fantasized about her countless times. Having her lay here beside me felt right. Easy. Comfortable. Last night I'd dreamed for the first time in years.

Staring at the ceiling gave me no answers. To be honest, I didn't even know the question. Something about this situation felt destined, and I didn't want to burst the perfect bubble.

Instead of keeping my mouth shut and enjoying the serenity, some random shit came out. "I don't remember crashing here last night."

Her gorgeous smile returned. "Clearly fate has a mind of her own."

She laughed, though it sounded a little higher pitched than usual. Nervous? Excited?

I paused a moment, catching my thoughts, trying to think of a topic that didn't involve thinking about her body draped over mine. Because right now, I couldn't concentrate on anything else.

Damn it. I had nothing.

She huffed a breath and flipped onto her back, squishing my arm underneath her neck. Once again, I was stuck. *Oh, well.*

"Fate seems to keep throwing obstacles in our way. Maybe we're only meant to be friends."

Utter bullshit. The connection between us was impossible to ignore. Believe me, I'd tried. Kali Preston had tattooed her name on my heart the second I saw her in Cedar Valley. She'd latched onto my soul and exploded it with light. Since then, my feelings had only grown, matured over the years, progressing from a teenage crush to hardcore rip-my-heart-to-pieces love. She was stunning, the most beautiful woman I'd ever seen and not just because of our bond. That only intensified the feelings that were already there.

I found my fated mate earlier than most, I was just too damn stupid to accept that gift with open arms. When I finally stopped and listened, it was too late.

But she had a point. The universe kept throwing obstacles between us. One day, I had faith it would all fall into place. "Everything happens when it's meant to."

I wasn't sure whether I truly believed that. Fate brought us together, two souls destined to exist as one, but the shit that kept us apart was my fault. I screwed-up. If I hadn't, things would be different. We'd be together. She'd be happy.

Back to staring at the ceiling. "I'm sorry I upset you last night."

"Don't," she whispered, turning on her side to face me again. "Stop blaming yourself, Brax. You can't keep doing that. Of course, kissing would bring all our emotions to the surface, especially after how our last kiss ended. I knew the risk. But I wanted to kiss you regardless."

My heart stilled. I'd screwed up so many times. She deserved someone better. A guy with his shit together, not just someone with the alpha blood running through his veins. But I couldn't let her go. Not again.

"It's hard not to blame myself. Everyone expects me to be like Dad, an alpha who the whole town respected. The whole damn shifter community respected him. And what did I do? Eighteen months into the role, I let Zac's bear wander too close to the boundary..." I closed my eyes, exhaling a ragged breath.

"What happened to Zac wasn't your fault. We thought a human shot his bear, but we now suspect that didn't happen. If a hunter came onto the property intending to kill, the only person who's to blame is that hunter."

This woman was so damn strong. I didn't know what I'd done to score her soul linked with mine. I'd never deserve it.

Her eyes peered upward while she thought. "Harry was a good man, Brax, but no one expects you to be him. You're your own person. Your own alpha. Sure, you left. But you know what? You're here now and that counts for something. Family sticks together. That's how we get through the tough times, Brax. We do it together."

I brushed my knuckles over her cheek. I should stop this, get the hell out of bed, and take a cold shower. Save us both. "I hate all the pain between us."

"Me too." She angled her face, allowing my hand to trail down the side of her neck. "But you don't need to shoulder it on your own. Let me in."

My list of shit to do today was endless. Yet, the only thing on my mind was touching Kali, kissing her, having her naked beneath me. Removing the giant canyon between us. But I'd vowed to keep my hands to myself until we extinguished the threat to our family.

How's that working out, asshole?

"Kiss me again."

Fuck. She did not just say that.

"I mean, as payment for sleeping in my bed uninvited."

Her voice turned playful, and my control slipped away damn fast.

My heart flipped around in my chest like a new cub with boundless energy. No idea how, considering all essential blood still hung out in my dick.

"*Your* bed, huh?"

"Yep. This is the room I'm staying in. Your room is downstairs. So technically, you snuck into my bed in the middle of the night."

Warning bells rang loud in my ears. Big fucking sirens. Flashing red and blue lights, horns sounding, and random flags waving at me to stop. Somehow, I doubted kissing Kali again would help our situation, nor would it aid in keeping the distance between us.

Of course, my fucking brain didn't function properly around her. "I suppose that's only fair."

Her eyes heated and my blood exploded into flames.

I didn't give a shit anymore. I'd made too many mistakes to count. Kissing Kali was never one of them. I wanted her more than my next breath.

Who was I to deny her? She requested payment for creeping into my—*her*—bed last night, and I always paid my debts. This time I'd make our kiss good for her. No tears.

I propped myself up on an elbow, half covering her body with mine. With one hand, I cupped her face and leaned in, hovering at her mouth. She drew in her bottom lip, wetting it, her scorching gaze locked on mine. My heart fucking flatlined.

Kali lifted her chin, and I closed the distance. First a soft kiss to one side of her mouth, then to the other, followed by a gentle, lingering kiss on her chin. I paused for a second before placing a kiss on her lips. Her mouth parted slightly, and I slid my tongue along the curve of her bottom lip, craving more of her taste. Kali slanted her head to capture my mouth with hers.

Things turned hazy after that. Our kiss deepened, became more urgent, our lips pressed harder together. A sweet moan exhaled from her mouth, sending a wild thrill through my body.

This kiss was like nothing else. Nothing like our first kiss, nor remotely like the one we shared in the study. This kiss felt stronger, more powerful. A sweet, silent, turning point. And if I thought the stars parted the first time we kissed, they had nothing on right now.

Did it scare the shit out of me? Abso-fucking-lutely. Did I stop and pull away? No fucking way. I kept careening toward that cliff, knowing damn well a big-ass world of pain awaited me over the edge.

Worth it.

She slid a palm around the back of my neck, holding me in place, locking our lips together. Our tongues explored, pushing and pulling, giving and taking. Kissing Kali heightened every sensation to an almost painful level.

Before things progressed too far—more than they

already had—I slowed down and eased back, hovering at her lips. By now, we were both a panting mess.

"Brax..."

I silenced her words with another kiss, deeper, drawn-out, ending in a nip on her bottom lip. Jesus, I was such a mess when it came to her.

Pure, raw heat swirled in her eyes. I couldn't speak. My throat suddenly dry.

"I want you," she whispered.

Her fingers trailed the outside of my shirt heading dangerously toward my jeans' zipper.

"Kal..." I tried to clear the lump in my throat. It wouldn't budge. "We can't take this further."

"Why? I'm a big girl, Brax. I can make my own decisions. We're both adults, and we both want this. At least, you seem to want this as much as I do."

Evident by my straining cock pressed against her thigh. "I do. It's just more complicated than that."

I didn't want to hurt her again. Sex would seal our mating bond, a connection she didn't even know existed. Of course I wanted her. I wanted her body plastered to mine for the rest of eternity.

Sneaky fingers hovered at the waistband of my jeans.

"Give me one good reason why we shouldn't."

My heart pounded beneath her touch. Once we sealed the mating bond, we couldn't undo it. I needed to tell her. I wouldn't trick her into a lifelong commitment just to sate a need.

"You're...my fated mate, Kal."

Her hand stilled. She remained silent. I felt better,

finally telling her the truth. It freed some pain inside me and lifted a weight off my shoulders. Hopefully now she understood why I left, why I couldn't stay and complete the mating bond with her after Zac died. She deserved better.

After the longest time, she whispered, "I always suspected."

Her hand ventured to my face, smoothing a path along my jaw, and trailed down to my collarbone.

"That's why I sense you a moment before you walk into a room. Why your bear responds to my voice. That explains the way your parents always looked at us like they counted down the days for us to get our act together."

"Subtlety isn't Mom's strongest quality."

Her chest quaked with a soft chuckle. "That's true."

She thought for a moment, her hand still trailing my collarbone and over my shoulder.

"I feel like our bond sealed the first time we kissed. Probably even before that. My heart has been yours since I saw you in that diner more than ten years ago. Having sex won't make some mystical connection feel any different. I'm already yours. I always have been."

My pulse wouldn't calm the fuck down.

She cupped my face with both hands.

"I want this with you, Brax. Let's stop punishing ourselves by denying us the right to be together. Let's have this one beautiful moment to rewrite our past. A moment we can cherish forever. We both deserve that."

I sure as hell wanted it, just wasn't sure I deserved it. "I can't promise to stay."

She nodded, though the spark in her eyes dimmed.

"I'm not asking you to stay. I'm only asking for right now."

I was the lowest type of scum because I wanted this even knowing afterward, she'd officially be my mate. Mating would bind us together for the rest of our lives.

I couldn't stay. She deserved more. But hell, what I wanted most of all was to give her the whole goddamn world.

chapter thirteen

Kali

I came undone the moment Brax grazed his chin along the sensitive spot on my neck. His stubble sent goosebumps bursting down the entire side of my body. Rough hands smoothed over my ribs, all the way down to my belly before slipping beneath the hem of my shirt. My body ached and burned in a way I couldn't comprehend. I'd had sex before, twice to be exact. Not with Brax, but an old boyfriend way before Brax confessed his feelings for me. The sex was all right, nothing to write home about. Nothing like this, and Brax and I weren't even naked yet.

Confirming I was his mate explained so much. Why his grumpy ass was so overly protective each time he saw me with said boyfriend. The poor guy wouldn't even step foot on the Archer property. I didn't blame him. Zac, Harley, and Levi weren't any better. It made having a boyfriend a little awkward.

I'd always considered Brax out of my league. Zac's best friend. Though, I never once saw Brax as a brother in the way I saw Harley and Levi. With Brax, everything had always felt...different. Heightened. Raw. Powerful. As though we had this magic brewing between us, patiently waiting for the day it would burst into the cosmos and change our lives forever. Now I knew why.

I mentally swore. We could've been naked so long ago if he'd only told me.

Brax positioned himself between my legs. Leaning forward, he slipped his arms underneath my back and lifted me to straddle his lap. Slowly, he slid my shirt up over my head, never once taking his intense gaze off me. This close to him, I could hardly breathe. Pant. *Whatever*.

I lost myself in his eyes, the way they darkened around the rim, how without ever saying a word, they saw right through mine to the heart of my soul. A heart-breaking combination of love, adoration, and awe reflected in those dark eyes, stealing my breath. I'd never recover from this.

Without a bra, my nipples pinched tight, breasts full and heavy with anticipation. He did this to me. This strong, gorgeous, half-broken man cradling me in his arms worshiped me with his eyes as though I were a mystical goddess. In this moment, I felt like one.

With slow and deliberate movements, he leaned in, trailing his tongue along my neck to my collarbone. My head fell back, giving him better access to the sensitive skin. One hand kneaded my breast, cupping it, circling his thumb over the peak. Little sparks of fireworks danced before my eyes. I was in so much trouble. At this rate, I'd fall apart the moment he removed my panties. Maybe even before that.

I needed him. I'd never needed something as much as I needed him. I ached for our bodies to not just join as one, but to have his flesh pressed against mine, our limbs tangled together, our hearts beating in unison. Our souls united.

My greedy hands clawed at the hem of his shirt. He eased his mouth from my neck and ripped it off, tossing it somewhere behind him. I didn't care where our clothes landed. We no longer needed them.

Oh, God. His chest. Sure, I'd seen him without a shirt before, but never this close. Never where I could appreciate and admire every peak and ridge of his glorious body. Following the lines of his tattoos, my fingers explored over the sculpted muscles along his pecs, his strong shoulders, his bulging biceps. He leaned back as my fingers dipped further down, following the thin trail of dark hair leading to the impressive bulge positioned between my legs. Every inch of him was absolute perfection.

Brax crooked a finger under my chin, tilting my head up.

"You're so beautiful."

If I wasn't already in love with the man, I would be now.

The look in his eyes was complete and utter sin. The kind of heated gaze that told me he didn't just want sex, he wanted to devour me.

Fine by me.

With his arms supporting me, he eased my back onto the bed once more. His fingers curved around my side, circling at my hips before he tucked them into the waistband of my panties.

He paused, looking up at me from between my legs. "I've wanted this, baby, for so long. But I need you to be sure."

His lips were swollen and pink from our kisses, his eyes so dark they bordered on black. I wasn't the only one affected here. But we were both too stubborn to admit it.

I nodded. How the hell did he expect me to speak?

"It's not something we can undo. If you have any doubts..."

His care, his words, how he still protected me in his own way even now, made my heart swell beyond belief. Even if I had doubts, which I didn't, he just erased them. I knew the repercussions of our actions. I knew that by having sex with him, I tied my soul to his for the rest of our lives. It didn't matter. Sex or not, mating bond or not, my heart and soul would always belong to Brax Archer. It always had.

I reached up and cupped his cheek. "I'm sure, Brax. I want this."

"Thank fuck. I would've stopped if you asked me to, but I'm fucking glad you didn't."

My giggle morphed into a moan when he wriggled down my panties. They flew in the air behind him like his shirt. Bye-bye clothes.

I raised on one elbow, watching him as he hopped off the bed and undressed. I swallowed. I mean, I thought his body was magnificent before. Now? I...had no words.

He crawled back between my legs.

"Do you have protection?" A baby at twenty-five wasn't ideal, especially if Brax bailed again and left me as a single parent with two overprotective uncles.

"Yep."

One finger slid down my center, and I collapsed into a tingling, gooey mess.

"I've dreamed of you naked. You're so goddamn beautiful."

"Really?" I panted, trying freaking hard to maintain some level of composure over my moaning.

"Mmm-hmm."

His finger circled my sensitive flesh before sliding down the center and easing inside me.

"*Oh.*" My eyes rolled back.

"You like that?" He repeated the motion, spending a little more time on each delicate spot.

"Hell, yeah. Don't stop."

A low growl rumbled from his chest, barely audible. "I don't plan to."

He continued caressing, torturing me in the most pleasurable way, sending me higher and higher to that blissful peak. If I died today, I'd die complete.

I angled my head to better watch him, watch me. His heated gaze locked on mine while his fingers stroked between my legs, coursing wave after wave of heat through my blood. That finger slipped inside me again, curling slightly, hitting a spot that sent a brilliant white-hot flash through my middle. My lids closed as my back arched.

Yep. I wouldn't last.

"Brax…" My mind shut down before I finished whatever I was about to say.

He scooted backward. With his fingers still exploring deep inside me, he lowered his mouth.

"Oh, my *God*." My back arched off the bed. The sensations, the touch, having Brax do wicked things with his mouth, all became too much. I knew he'd wreck me if his tongue touched another part of my body. I was so right.

He sucked, nipped, and stroked like I was his freaking savior. Maybe I was. A faint voice inside my head whispered that he was also mine.

Bolts of lightning shot from every direction crashing into me. My head thrashed side to side, wanting him to finish me, but also wanting this to last forever. His fingers pumped a steady rhythm, working me higher and higher while his tongue lapped.

One of my hands clutched the bed linen, bunching it in my grasp. The other curled in his hair, tugging, holding him in place. His low growl rumbled louder as his tongue worked me even harder, sucking deep pulls. My thighs squeezed around his head, rocking against his mouth, desperate for release.

His tongue licked feverishly, sending me careening over the edge of that cliff into a pool of bliss. No, not a pool. He sent me to freaking heaven. My body had never been so high and had never fallen so hard. I had him to thank for that. Best orgasm of my freaking life.

Tiny light aftershocks pulsed between my legs as my breath punched in and out. I vaguely registered him rolling on a condom before he lifted me onto his lap.

"I've ached to taste you. To mate with you."

His hands dug into my ass, rubbing his hard length along the outside of my wetness, sending new waves of fire through my middle.

"I want this to be perfect for you."

My heart flopped out of my chest and died right there beside me on the bed.

I scraped my nails up the nape of his neck into his thick hair. "It is perfect. It couldn't be more perfect."

The familiar pain behind my heart reared its ugly head, threatening to ruin the moment. I wouldn't let it. I wanted this. Even if Brax left again, plummeting me into a miserable pit of despair and heartbreak, it would be worth it. We needed this. After so many years of longing for each other, we deserved this.

One hot night with Brax freaking Archer. To hell with self-preservation.

I rolled my hips, sliding along the outside of his hardness. "I need you inside me."

He took my mouth in a fevered kiss. The taste of me on his tongue started off weird but ended up a downright turn-on. I moaned. I couldn't help it. It totally worked in my favor because Brax deepened our kiss.

In no time, our kiss turned hungry and wet with a fierceness that made me melt. He lifted my butt, and with one hand between us, positioned himself at my entrance. Slowly, he slid me down on top of him. My entire world fell to pieces. Tiny, shattered, beautiful pieces. Pinpricks of light erupted before my eyes, a dazzling display of beauty while heat raged through my veins.

He stretched and filled me until the most delicious combination of sensations threatened to explode in my soul. Buried fully inside me, he drew back slightly to look at me, his fingers digging into my butt cheeks holding me in place. The desire in his gaze stole my breath. So wild, full of emotion and unsaid words. I'd never seen this side of him. For one sweet moment, all his walls crumbled, and he let me peek into his most guarded, hidden feelings. He was wrong to leave, his mesmerizing eyes told me. I meant something to him, despite the fact he left.

Before I caught it all, his walls slammed back up and he began moving inside me. Gentle at first, slow and deep, making my freaking eyes roll back in my head.

The grip on my butt tightened as he rocked. Scorching, wet kisses trailed down my neck, sending tiny shivers along my spine. The tempo increased as his fingers dug deeper. I'd probably have tiny circular bruises tomorrow, and I didn't care. I grabbed the back of his head, holding his mouth against my collarbone and got with the program, rocking back and forth. Harder. Deeper.

Brax growled, sucked, and nipped along my shoulder, once again building me higher and higher. Little beads of sweat slid between us, tingling my nipples as they rubbed up and down his firm chest.

I didn't care if this was a one-night thing. Being with Brax was hands down the best moment of my life. Nothing compared.

When the pace became too fast, Brax flipped me onto my back, lifting one leg as he pounded into me. Every firm muscle in his body tightened and contracted in a glorious display. His face set in fierce hard lines, his intense dark gaze locked on me.

I lost control. Brax thrusting inside me, digging his fingers into my thighs, the emotion in his eyes, the heady smell of sex filling the room. I couldn't take it any longer. A ball of light expanded deep inside me, filling and swelling until it exploded in a giant flash of searing heat. A supernova. My core pulsed again and again, gripping him inside me. Brax groaned, pumping harder. One more deep thrust and his powerful body shuddered, coming apart inside me.

My mind and body checked out, drifted off to that blissful plane of post-orgasm land somewhere between here and heaven. I'd never be the same.

After what seemed like hours, Brax withdrew, disposed of the condom, and collapsed on the bed beside me. He wrapped me in his arms, his chest rising and falling with heavy breaths. A swell of satisfaction, maybe even a little evil dose of power, surged through me. I did that to him. I made him lose control like that. Little old me.

His mate.

We lay there for a while longer, staring at the ceiling as our breathing steadied, and my pulse returned to a somewhat normal rhythm.

"You were right," he murmured, drawing me even tighter.

I lifted my head, still not able to move the rest of my body. "About what?"

"Our mate bond." He stared at the ceiling, inhaling a slower breath before peering down at me in the crook of his arm. "Sealing it didn't...change anything."

Something heavy slammed onto my chest, crushing my lungs. I rested my cheek back on his chest and snuggled into his warmth while the ache in my heart moved front and center. Even though I told myself it didn't matter, that I'd survive without him, part of me hoped sex would strengthen our bond, heighten it somehow. That in some twisted way, it would awaken Brax's feelings, so he'd choose to stay. But he'd always felt our bond, it had always been there, and he'd still left.

I closed my eyes as a rush of emotion threatened to spill. What if this time was no different?

chapter fourteen

Brax

I drummed my fingers on the kitchen counter, watching the circle of batter in the pan, waiting for it to bubble. I swear to God the pancake cooked slower the more I stared at it. By now though, I was fully committed to the stare-off and wouldn't back down. The damn pancake would bubble any second.

Levi strode into the kitchen, heading to the fridge. "You were up early. I ducked my head into the guest room, but you weren't there." He opened the fridge to grab the juice carton.

I ignored the little punk's questioning tone. Whether

I made it to the guest room last night was none of his business. "Yep. Went for a run." Staring at the frypan made lying a shitload easier.

"Right." Glass and juice in hand, Levi plonked himself at the table across from Kali. "You go for a run too, Kali-belly? Your cheeks look a little...flushed."

Asshole. I spun, ready to smack the back of Levi's head but lucky for him, I refrained. Like a needy toddler, he craved a reaction, and I wouldn't give him the satisfaction. Kali did well not to choke on her mouthful of breakfast or throw a knife at him. She raised her brows and nodded, chewing a little slower.

Back to the stove. Bubbles finally appeared in the batter, and I flipped the pancakes. Levi helped himself to a stack and the bacon piled in the center of the table. Food should shut him up for a while. His mouth ran like a tap some days.

When the last batch was ready, I tossed them onto the plate and returned to the table, sitting beside Kali. Where I belonged.

"I'm glad our seating arrangements have returned to normal," Levi bitched around a mouthful of food. "Yesterday confused the hell outta me."

I ignored him, piling bacon on top of my pancake before drowning it in maple syrup. Maple syrup and I were in a committed relationship.

Harley stormed into the kitchen and snatched a piece of bacon. "Some asshole broke into the garage last night. I'm heading into town to assess the damage."

Acid churned in my stomach. This nightmare wouldn't fucking end. In the blissful hours of this morning with Kali curled in my arms, I almost forgot about the threat that lured me home. I'd also nearly forgotten my intention to leave.

I needed to end this so Kali and I could figure out where we stood. Because I was damn sure that if she asked me to stay, I would in a heartbeat.

The espresso machine gurgled as Harley brewed a coffee in a takeout mug. I should go with him to the garage, but I couldn't bring myself to move.

Kali's gentle hand on my thigh drew my attention. "Go with him."

"I don't want to leave you, not with your dad in town."

"I'm safe here." She gave my thigh a light squeeze. "This is who you are, Brax Archer. Stop fighting it."

A big-ass lump closed my throat. Part of me didn't want to leave Kali's side, but the other didn't want to pretend to be something I wasn't. Alpha of Cedar Valley. The role I was born for, the one Dad had groomed me for since I was a kid. The birthright I walked away from two years ago. But Kali was right. This was me. Eliminating this latest threat wouldn't cure my demons, nor would it rewrite my past mistakes. But I sure as hell wouldn't allow someone else to die. Not on my watch.

The time for sitting on the sidelines was over.

I curled my hand around the nape of Kali's neck, drawing her closer so I could kiss her forehead, lingering for a moment while I breathed in her scent. To hell if my brothers saw.

Releasing her, I pushed back from the table, stood,

and shoved a decent fork full of maple syrup drenched pancake in my mouth. "I'll come."

Harley nodded, filling another takeout mug with coffee. "Meet you in the truck."

I placed my plate in the sink and turned to Levi. "Call me..." *If anything happens.*

I hoped my look conveyed the unsaid words. My heart couldn't stomach saying them aloud.

Levi tipped his chin in silent agreement. He was a smartass, but he also knew when to be serious.

Harley drove us to the garage on the main street of town. The three of us owned equal parts in the business, though Levi wasn't a qualified mechanic. He worked behind the scenes, doing the books. Things Harley and I avoided at all costs. Being shifters didn't exempt us from human taxes, especially if we wanted to blend into their world.

We parked around the back, entering through the rear door.

"Jesus," I muttered.

The place was a fucking shit storm. Tools strewn over the concrete floor. So much oil splashed over the walls that the slightest spark would blow up the entire place. I trudged farther into the garage, stepping over the spilled grease, heading to the priceless possession parked on the far side. A thick, sour taste filled my mouth the closer I came. Usually, a sheet draped the ruby red Camaro, but not today. Some asshole ripped it off and took to the car with a hammer. Smashed glass littered the floor, and so many tiny dints covered the usually smooth, glossy paint. It now resembled a fucking golf ball.

This car was Dad's pride and joy. A hobby project he'd shared with me and Harley since we were cubs. He never drove the damn thing, always insisted on fixing something else, but that was beside the point.

Destroying this car made shit personal.

If it turned out that Kali's father was a hunter, and he targeted my pack, I'd make sure the fucker died by my hand.

"I'll kill them, Brax. I'll tear their limbs right off their bodies," Harley growled, inspecting the damage.

"Get in line."

I trailed my hand along the hood, my boots crunching the broken glass as I walked to the other side. "Something doesn't feel right. First the text, then the shifter blood, now this. It doesn't add up."

"I feel it, too."

I looked at Harley from across the hood. "If Kali's father is behind this, why do all this shit? Why not just attack?"

"I dunno, Brax. But it's time we found out."

Best idea ever.

I grabbed my cell and made a few calls to the neighboring packs, but once again, no one else had reported any damage. Nor had they spotted any hunters in the area. After cleaning up the garage, I'd shift and search the woods for any sign of Jack Preston. Something told me this was all him and it wouldn't stop until we ended him.

Harley's apprentice, who called in the damage, arrived with cleaning supplies and we got to work. I tried to push aside the churning in my lower gut. Things didn't add up. Why the hell would a hunter destroy a garage? Why not target the house? Or the actual shifters that lived there?

Without realizing it, the hours flew by. For almost a second, I didn't think of my responsibilities, my past mistakes, or the front-page feature on my latest screw-up: mating with Kali. I was such an asshole. What if she didn't feel the same? What if sealing our bond didn't change things for her? I should've spoken to her this morning instead of basking in her light and warmth, and our post-sex bliss.

To top it off, my words came out all wrong. Like hell our bond didn't feel any different. I just didn't know how to describe it. I didn't think anything could make me love her more than I already did but sealing our bond launched that love to a whole new level. Into a new stratosphere. I should've said that to her. Told her that the bond didn't magically create feelings. I'd already placed my soul in the palm of her hand years ago. But words weren't my thing. They always came out like a jumbled mess around Kali.

Cleaning the garage gave me the headspace to realize what I wanted deep down. The answer was always Kali Preston. With her by my side, everything else would fall into place.

Steady rain beat down on the roof, adding extra bass to the rock music Harley blared from a Bluetooth speaker. Mid-afternoon, my cell buzzed in my back pocket and I grabbed it out to answer it. Levi's number flashed on the screen. "Yeah?"

"Brax, get back here."

I froze. "What?"

"My buddy on the force rang. He traced the number."

"And? Fucking spit it out, Levi."

Levi's voice sounded muffled like he cupped his hand over the phone. "Here. The cell is here on the property. Right now."

My heart plummeted through the concrete floor. "Harley," I shouted, waving him over as I raced to the truck with the cell still at my ear. "Don't let Kali out of your fucking sight, do you hear me?"

"I won't."

I threw the phone on the dash and started the truck. Harley barely made it in the passenger side before I skidded out of the parking lot.

chapter fifteen

Kali

"Ugh. Tell me what's going on," I snapped at Levi.

Yet again, my pestering went unanswered. The guy raced around the house locking windows and shutting doors but refused to tell me why. Clearly, not good news on the other end of his phone call.

I stood in the doorway, hands on hips and planted my feet firmly on the floor, shoulder-width apart. If Levi wanted out of the bedroom, he'd need to shove me aside. Given our size difference, he could easily, but he wouldn't. Hopefully. When he moved to slip around me, I stepped in his way. Hard lines and deep creases over his forehead replaced his usual relaxed, funny-guy expression. I'd only seen Levi this worked up once. No, twice. When his dad died and when Zac...

Dread plummeted deep in my gut. The hunter. I felt it with every fiber in my body.

I jutted out my chin. "I'm not a child. Tell me."

He stared at me for a moment, his gaze darting between the staircase and me as though he considered lifting me out of his way and making a run for it. Instead, he exhaled a defeated breath. "My buddy on the force just called. The cell that sent the text is on the property. Now."

"Who? Who is it?"

His eyes flashed with black as his bear threatened to shift. "It's a burner phone. But...let's not rule out anyone."

Meaning, my father.

Air whooshed from my lungs making me dizzy. Sure, ever since Harley spotted Jack in town, I'd suspected his involvement. But...to know that whoever sent the text was now on the property...a thousand questions flooded my mind. Mainly I wanted to know why. Why did they send it? Did they slaughter that shifter at the garage?

Was it my father?

I wanted the truth, but perhaps not that last answer.

"Brax and Harley are heading back. I..."

I snapped out of my daze. "You what?"

I could hardly hear him over the pulse rushing in my ears.

"I think the break in at the garage was a diversion. Whoever it is needed Brax and Harley...away from us."

"Oh, God."

My knees buckled. Levi gripped my shoulders holding me steady.

"Why?"

He bent until we were at eye level. "The why doesn't matter. What matters is that I won't let anything happen to you. Now's not the time to panic. We need to arm ourselves. Brax keeps a gun in his room. Get it and meet me downstairs."

Arm myself? As in prepare to shoot someone? One of the first things Harry Archer taught Zac and I was how to use a gun for emergencies. I'd fired one before, but never at a living target. I couldn't even stomach the thought of shooting a person. Taking a life, no matter the reason, didn't feel right to me. But if it came to a choice between my life and some lowlife, would I be able to pull the trigger? What if it was my father?

I shook my head. "I can't..."

"Yes, you can, Kali. You're one of the strongest women I know. All we need to do is hold the fort until help gets here. One coward is no match for three bears. Get the gun and meet me in the living room."

Levi slipped past me and darted down the stairs. I didn't move. I couldn't. I stood there, every muscle frozen in place.

Six days ago, I'd received a text from an unknown number stating Zac's death wasn't an accident. Someone murdered him. Now, the sender was out there on the property. Why? And how did they know Zac's death wasn't an accident?

"Kali!" Levi shouted from the bottom of the stairs, startling me. "Hurry up."

I clenched my fist, drawing all my anger and frustration into one tight ball, spinning it into adrenaline to snap myself into action. I could do this. Levi and I could do this. He was right, we just needed to hold the fort until Brax and Harley returned.

I just hoped they weren't too late.

"I'm coming," I growled.

I rushed into Brax's bedroom, threw open the drawers searching for a gun. No luck. I checked under the bed. Nope. Inside the closet, I flicked on the light and tossed aside clothes searching. There. Up on the highest shelf I spotted the handgun. Not sure how I felt about it being in the room the entire time, but I'd save that conversation for later.

Without wasting another second, I loaded it, tucked the gun into the back of my jeans and ran downstairs. Having a weapon digging into my tailbone wasn't as comfortable as it looked in the movies. Action heroes made everything look so easy.

I skidded to a halt in the living room as Levi peeked out the window from behind the drapes. He had a gun tucked in his jeans also, but he seemed much more comfortable with it. Letting go of the drapes, he turned to me, his eyes a dark shade of brown, bordering on black.

My heart thrummed so hard in my chest. The air so heavy and intense in the room, it squeezed my lungs, suffocating me with an invisible force. Was Brax close? I needed to sit before I—

A gunshot cracked outside, making me squeal.

"Shh." Levi held a finger to his lips, glaring at me.

I glared back. What did he expect me to do?

A gunshot sounded again, from the same direction as the first. Levi peeked between the drapes again. With the rain pelting down outside, I doubt he saw more than a few feet from the house.

"I need to go outside to see how many there are."

I gaped at him. He was the youngest Archer, but was he really that stupid? "No way. I've watched enough horror movies to know you shouldn't leave the house to investigate a noise. In fact, we should call the cops. Can't you call your buddy again? Tell him to send help?"

"He already alerted the shifter authorities and requested backup. But we can't involve the human cops. The last thing we need is them showing up on the scene and having a bear attack."

Knowing help was on the way should've eased my panic. But something Levi said made my pulse spike. What if there was more than one attacker? What if it was my father? What if he wasn't alone? "When will help arrive?"

Those creases returned to Levi's brow, and his gaze darted to the back door. "They're on their way."

A weight sank low in my belly. Help wouldn't arrive quickly enough. I received that message loud and clear.

Another shot rang out, still from the same direction only louder this time. We both turned toward the sound. This was it. The turning point where we had to either fight or fall. Help wouldn't get here in time. If we wanted to survive, we needed to face the threat on our own. I wasn't ready, but I had to be. I had to stand tall and put all those years of training into practice.

I wasn't a shifter, but I was part of the Archer pack. And I wouldn't let this lunatic ruin everything I held dear.

My gaze locked with Levi's, finding a similar sense of determination in his eyes. I knew what we needed to do. We couldn't sit here and wait.

I gave him a curt nod.

Before I said anything, Levi raced to the back door.

"Stay here. I'll find out how many there are and come right back. Aim that gun at this door and don't open it for anyone but me. Understand?"

I was too numb to do anything but nod.

Once he slipped outside, I closed the door and engaged the deadlock. Backing up a few steps, I stared at the door, gun held low and tight. Blood thrashed in my ears. My hearing soared into overdrive, picking up even the quietest sounds. Rain, creaks on the roof, distant rumbles of thunder.

I waited. Listened. Waited some more. Minutes flew by until my hand ached, wrapped too tight around the butt of the handgun. Levi should've been back by now. What took him so long?

Another gunshot made me jolt. This time the sound came from the opposite side of the property.

Where the hell was Levi? I shouldn't have let him leave. Even if Brax sped, it still took at least twenty minutes to get here from town. If anything happened to Levi...

My stomach sank. The entire thing was a setup.

Divide and conquer. Send the stronger Archer brothers into town, so the attacker could prey on the weaker, smaller. Levi wasn't weak, but he was the youngest brother. And he'd just walked headfirst into a trap.

If he shifted, he could defend himself, but human form was better for tracking. Bears excelled at fighting and physical combat, but they weren't predators. Not like wolves.

To take out an attacker, we needed to think like one. We needed to hunt.

Rolling my feet, I crept to the window and peeked between the gap in the drapes. The rain made it near impossible to see anything except sheets of water. Angry storm clouds blanketed the sky, bringing early darkness. I couldn't see past the porch, let alone farther out to spot Levi or his bear.

Closing the drapes once more, I retreated from the window until my back flattened against the far wall facing the back door.

Something heavy thumped on the porch. My hand tightened around the gun, lifting it to point at the door. I stilled. Held my breath. Was it Levi? Was his bear outside? Twisting sideways, I cocked my ear toward the door and listened, but the furious rain drowned out too many sounds. I waited a few more seconds. When nothing else happened, I curled my free hand around the knob. My heart raced. A big, thick mass clawed its way up my throat.

I could do this. I wasn't weak. I would step up and fight to protect this pack. My family.

I turned the handle and inched it open, slipping the

muzzle of the gun in the crack between the door and frame. Leaning to one side, I peeked through the gap.

Levi lay face down on the porch, a few feet from the door. His head lifted as I opened the door wider, his eyes wild and fierce.

"Kali...*run*."

The words barely left his mouth before his cheek smacked the floor.

Instinct made me throw open the door and rush to him. I dropped to my knees beside his head, placing the gun down.

"Levi."

I grabbed his shoulder to rouse him but recoiled when I spotted the black-handled hunting knife lodged in his back.

Oh, God. Someone stabbed him.

He whimpered. A voice in the back of my head yelled at me to go back inside the house. Being out here on the porch made us targets.

I reached to yank out the blade but stilled with my hand around the hilt. If I did that, would it make the bleeding worse or better? Letting go, I shuffled closer to get a better look. Darkness seeped through his shirt, pooling around the blade. What did I do? Take it out or leave it? Provided the blade didn't puncture his heart or lungs...or any vital organ for that matter, he should survive. His shifter blood would heal him. But if we both stayed here on the porch, whoever stabbed him could attack again.

We could both die.

Dizziness threatened to sweep me under, but I refused to sink.

Focus, Kali.

I needed to get us inside, away from immediate danger. After that, I'd deal with the blade. Maybe then, Brax and Harley would be here.

I shuffled to Levi's head and lifted into a crouched position before grabbing both his hands to stretch out his arms. He grunted. Whimpered again.

"It's okay, Levi. I'm going to take you inside."

I straightened and used all my strength to pull—

Something caught my attention through the sheets of rain. I froze, scanning the forest.

A hooded figure stepped from the tree line. My heart sank.

The rain hindering my vision didn't make a difference. Something deep inside my soul recognized the figure.

My father.

chapter sixteen

Brax

I drove as fast as the truck would take us without sliding off the road and into a ditch. Storms were common in the valley, but not like this. It hadn't rained this heavily for years. Of all the days.

Harley lowered the cell from his ear. "They're not answering."

"Fuck." I slammed my palm against the steering wheel. Harley dialed Levi again, but I didn't expect a different result.

I veered off the highway onto the dirt road, the back tires

slid out in a wide arc, forcing me to spin in the other direction to hold it steady. How I kept all four wheels on the road was a miracle. The muddy drive wound through the forest for a good half mile before it reached the ranch. Almost there.

"We need to presume Kali's father is involved." I skidded around another bend with the precision of an elite rally driver. Harley braced his forearm on the passenger window. Mud and rocks flung up under the tray. The windshield wipers panicked, swishing faster than the tires spun, attempting to clear the water enough for me to see. It didn't work. Darkness consumed this part of the forest on a sunny day, let alone one filled with torrential fucking rain.

"They could be in the cellar without their cells."

Harley. Always the optimist.

I grunted. Preventing us from slamming into a tree was more important than debating my point.

Just before the forest cleared, I slid the truck to a stop in the middle of the road and killed the engine. My heart raced. Kali was inside the house, probably terrified. I had one chance to save her. One chance to end this for good. I couldn't screw it up.

"What's the plan?"

I unbuckled my seatbelt. "We hunt. We'll leave the truck here and shift. You head around the west, I'll take the east, we'll meet up at the rear."

Harley twisted in his seat to face me. "Shifting is risky, Brax. We can't carry a gun in bear form. We'll rely solely on our bears to fight."

Captain Obvious.

When it came to protecting my mate, my family, I'd do fucking anything.

"I know. But our bears are faster and stealthier than this damn truck. If we drive out of the forest toward the ranch, we'll expose our position. If it's Jack Preston, he could be anywhere. And what if he's not alone? What if there's a shitload of hunters surrounding the house? We have no idea what the situation is. That's a bigger risk than shifting and relying on our bears."

After a few precious seconds, Harley nodded. "You're right. Let's end these fuckers." He unbuckled his belt, pulled his shirt over his head, and tossed it on the floor. "How close is Rhett's pack?"

"Not close enough."

Harley held my gaze for a heartbeat. An overwhelming urge to thank him swelled in my chest. To thank him for keeping the pack together in my absence, for protecting Kali, for doing everything I should've when I was too lost in self-pity to realize it. But the words stalled in my throat.

Harley squeezed his firm hand on my shoulder. "Keep me updated."

I gave him a curt nod. While in bear form, we could mentally communicate. Not in full conversations like talking in human form, but short snippets of words. Enough to get the point across. Enough to alert others in the pack of danger or the whereabouts of a hunter.

Harley opened the door and got out of the truck, and I did the same. Rain drenched my clothes. I stripped, throwing the soaked clothing onto the truck floor along with my boots before slamming the door shut.

A gunshot cracked through the forest, coming from near the house. I stilled, catching Harley's wide-eyed gaze over the hood. Although hunters possessed increased speed and strength, they often used weapons to immobilize their prey before draining their blood. Most weren't stupid enough to attack with their bare hands.

We were out of time. My pack, my mate was out there unprotected. I wouldn't fail them again.

"Let's do this," I growled.

Harley's body contorted. His back bowed. Bones cracked and fused. In less than a second, he shifted into a grizzly. His bear peered back at me before darting deep into the forest.

Buck naked, I raced in the opposite direction and mentally relinquished control. My bear, ready and eager to protect his mate, busted free from his cage. In one swift movement, I shifted mid-stride with a single objective front and center in my mind: save her.

chapter seventeen

Kali

My first instinct was to run. I'd seen what this man could do and how he savagely attacked my brother right before my eyes. But I wasn't that timid little girl anymore. I knew about the shifter world, and I'd spent the last ten years of my life living with a pack of bears. My mate was Mr. Alpha Bear. That counted for something. Surely.

Fierce strength soared from some hidden place deep inside me. A powerful force to protect my family at any cost.

I clenched my jaw and tightened my grip on Levi's wrists.

How dare this man turn up here after more than ten years and threaten everything I held dear?

As though he sensed my determination, my father skulked back into the forest. He either mocked me or wanted me to chase him. Maybe he hid, waiting for Brax or Harley, suspecting we'd alerted them to the danger. Either way, I was done. So done. That man gave me life, but I sure as hell wouldn't let him take it away.

With another brutal yank, I heaved Levi inside the house and dropped his arms with a thud. The guy looked so much lighter. I wouldn't make that mistake again. Bracing my hands on my knees, I caught my breath while I eyed the blade stabbed in his back. The only way for Levi's shifter blood to heal him was for me to remove the knife. A wound couldn't seal with an object still lodged between the flesh.

Kneeling, I fought through the churning in my stomach and curled my fingers around the handle, ever so slowly sliding out the blade. The second the tip breached the surface, I tossed it on the floor away from me.

I lifted Levi's shirt, wriggling it up to inspect the wound. As though in slow motion, the blood eased until it stopped. Slower still, the flesh around the gash began to change color. Angry, dark red blotches lightened as the skin stitched itself back together. I breathed a freaking sigh as relief flooded me. Levi would live. He'd be fine.

But as that relief washed over me, something darker, more powerful surged through my veins, craving vengeance. Not just for injuring Levi, but for terrorizing this family. My family.

I peeled myself off the floor. Levi groaned. I didn't wait a second longer. Like Brax, Levi would stop me for sure. I threw open the door, swept the gun up off the floor and took off in the direction where I'd seen my father disappear.

By the time I reached the forest, my entire body trembled with shivers, my soaked clothes clung tight to my skin, but I kept running. Hunting the hunter. Entering the forest, I slowed my steps and veered right, guided by instinct or an invisible force I couldn't explain. Thick intertwined branches lightened the rain, making it easier to see, but they also blocked most of the light. Deep inside the forest, it now resembled night.

I darted around a large pine tree and slammed my back against the wide trunk as I orientated myself. Growing up, I'd explored this forest so many times. When Brax had shifted, I'd wander beside his bear as though we were best friends out for a stroll in the woods. In some way, I guess we were. Other times, I'd meander the forest alone, lost in thought, seeking the stillness and contentment only these trees provided.

I knew these woods better than my father.

Hidden behind the trunk, I listened for movement. For someone tracking me. Nothing. Only rain and distant rumbling thunder. Not even the purr of an engine or skidding tires.

By now, Brax should've reached the ranch, yet I hadn't heard his truck. And in the chaos, I left my cell inside the house. Too bad. No way I'd go back for it now. All I needed was the gun clutched in my hand.

Leaning to one side, I peeked around the trunk then repeated the motion in the other direction. No one. Which way did he go?

I sucked in a sharp breath. What if my father waited until I left so he could kill Levi? If he was a hunter, he'd crave shifter blood more than...me.

Shit.

I needed to go back.

God, this was a bad horror movie. Every time I watched one, I yelled at the characters' reckless choices, and I just did the same.

Instead of backtracking, doing a wide sweep through the forest made more sense, so I came around the house from the opposite side. That way, if my father was inside, I could sneak up on him.

With a deep breath, I pushed off the trunk and ran, curving up the mountain.

An arm darted out, bashing into my throat. My legs flung out and my back slammed on the ground with a sickening crunch. Air punched from my lungs. Heat exploded down my spine. The gun flung from my hand, lost in the undergrowth.

A blurry figure loomed over me. "Only cowards run."

Ice skated down my spine at my father's voice.

Warm, thick liquid pooled at the back of my skull, the sharp sting intensified, but I buried the pain. I wasn't a coward. I would face this man on both feet and end this terror once and for all.

I peeled myself off the ground and locked my shaky legs in place, shoulder-width apart.

"Why?" I couldn't think of another, more logical question.

Jack—because I refused to acknowledge a family link to him any longer—waved a knife in the air. "Why? I came for what's owed to me."

Dizziness washed over me, and I stumbled backward, but caught my balance. "What?"

The man before me was my father, but he resembled nothing but the nightmarish monster that tried to murder my brother. His eyes were bright amber. Narrow black slits replacing his pupils confirmed my fears. His shoulder-length hair was unkempt, ragged as though he'd lived in the woods for the past ten years like a rabid animal.

He prowled forward, his lip curling in a vicious snarl.

I glanced at the hunting knife gripped in his hand. Identical to the one I pulled from Levi's back. Did he have a matching set?

Clearly, I had a concussion, and hysteria took over.

"You're owed nothing." I blinked several times, clearing the patch of darkness dotting my vision. "You gave up all your rights when you tried to strangle me."

"I'm owed blood."

Bile rose in my throat. Not any blood. He craved shifter blood. Realization sank low and heavy in my gut. My father was a hunter. Brax had told me, hell, even I suspected it, but seeing it for myself felt so...final. He hadn't wanted to just murder Zac, he'd wanted his blood.

"I won't let you hurt anyone else."

He threw his head back and laughed. "You think you

can stop me?" His eyes narrowed. "Your mother once thought the same."

I gasped. "You didn't..."

Oh, God. I couldn't even stomach the thought.

"She did this to me." For a split second his eyes flashed a deep brown. Seeing the resemblance to Zac tore a fresh gash in my heart. "I was a powerful witch, descendent from a respectable line. Your mother hid her true form from me in the beginning. She tricked me into thinking she loved me." He waved the knife in the air. "Then she turned me into...this."

Either Jack was delusional, or my head injury was worse than I thought. A little of both?

"My mother didn't do this to you. A hunter has to kill, to drink the blood of a shifter to activate the curse." I covered my mouth as I staggered back. "You...killed her. You drank her blood."

He killed my mother. He'd told us she died when I was born, and I never questioned it. As kids, every time we asked about her, pain consumed his eyes until it became unbearable to watch. Eventually, we stopped talking about her altogether.

"This is her fault," he yelled.

This guy wasn't my father. He was bat-shit crazy. Or...lost to blood lust. Of course. I'd heard about it over the years. When hunters drank so much shifter blood, they went beyond craving immortality and heightened strength to outright blood lust.

A few feet to my left, I spotted my gun in a patch of wet leaves.

"You're crazy," I whispered, sidestepping toward the gun.

"I'm here for the alpha blood I need to cure what she did to me."

Hysteria set in and I laughed. "Newsflash. I'm not a shifter. Let alone an alpha."

He took a menacing step toward me, a sickening snarl curled on his lip. "No. But your brother was."

Oh, God. It all made sense. Ten years ago, he tried to kill Zac for his blood, to cure the hunter curse somehow. Honestly, I didn't even know if that worked.

"Zac's dead."

No reaction. Not even a flinch. Of course not, because he already knew. He sent the text after all.

I crept one small step at a time to the gun, ready to end this.

"When I tracked you and your brother to Cedar Valley and found you with Harry Archer, a rare opportunity presented itself. One I couldn't pass up. What's more potent than alpha blood? The product of two alphas." He flipped the knife in his hand. "I let him take you both in and I waited, bidding my time for the eldest Archer boy to become alpha. For his pure blood to intensify so it not only cured the curse but gave me more power than I ever dreamed of."

My eyes widened. No longer did he talk of Zac. He'd hid in the shadows waiting to kill...Brax.

The text. The diversions. Using me as bait.

"You sent a text for me to bring Brax home." I crept closer, the gun now within reach.

Behind Jack, a large gray wolf hunched low to the

ground, stalking between the trees toward us, its footsteps concealed by the rain. For some strange reason, I sensed the wolf wasn't a threat to me, only Jack. The wolf curled its top lip, revealing long, sharp fangs. Its ice-blue eyes locked on Jack's back.

If I kept my father distracted, I suspected the wolf would help take him down.

"Threatening the life of a shifter's mate is a powerful motivator."

"What about Zac? Did you kill him, too? Why bother when you wanted Brax?"

Jack glared at me. His eyes so full of hatred it made my stomach churn.

"It should've been that Archer boy. He was meant to be in the woods that night. But then the coward ran away just like Zac. So I lured him back."

Bile rose in my throat as I connected all the dots. Although different species, Zac's and Brax's bears were similar colors and around the same size. From a distance, especially at night, someone unfamiliar with their bears would have difficulty telling them apart.

My blood ran hot. I focused my rage on Jack, the psycho who took Zac from me and then used me to lure Brax to his death. "You bastard," I screamed.

"It should've been him."

Jack ripped a gun from behind his back as a grizzly bear prowled between the trees toward us, teeth bared, a murderous glint in his eyes.

Brax.

I couldn't allow an ounce of relief. We were all in

danger, and I'd no idea what Jack would do next. This ended now before he hurt someone else.

The bear snarled, lifted on hind legs, and growled a loud, thunderous warning. Brax intended to tear apart Jack, but I couldn't let that happen. He already had one death on his conscience. Another would break him even if this death was in retribution for the first. Even if Jack deserved to die.

I wouldn't let Brax shoulder this alone.

Jack aimed the gun at Brax. "How stupid of you to fight in bear form, without weapons. You really are a failed alpha. I'm doing the world a favor."

Jack Preston raised the gun, preparing to shoot.

He deserved to die. Not my brother. And certainly not my mate.

White-hot rage bubbled deep inside me, building and swelling until it consumed every cell and molecule of my body. My insides quaked, pulsed with a need for vengeance. Images flashed through my mind. My back bowed. Red dots appeared in my vision. A vicious growl rumbled from deep in my chest.

Everything happened at once. I dove for the gun. The gray wolf launched into the air. Brax's bear attacked. A single shot cracked through the forest.

chapter eighteen

Brax

I mages flashed through my mind, black and white snippets of the events right before my bear gave back control. *Charging at Jack Preston...Kali diving for something...her shifting...a wolf latching onto Jack's throat.*

All in one split second. I shifted back so damn quick.

By my feet, a large gray wolf snarled and tore at Jack's flesh, efficient at making that asshole dead. Two more wolves joined the first, one with reddish fur, the other dirty white, and they worked together to drag Jack's body out from under a motionless black bear. They snarled and growled as they tugged the lifeless hunter deeper into the forest.

Kali.

My knees hit the ground. "Kali? Baby, can you hear me?"

Her bear returned a low, painful whine.

I smoothed my hand along her glossy black fur, checking for injuries. A warm patch of wetness coated her underbelly. My heart lodged deep in my throat. A gun. Snippets of Kali swiping a gun off the ground flashed in my mind, right before she shifted. Then her bear launched between Jack and me.

She finally shifted, and someone fucking shot her.

Just like Zac.

I didn't protect her.

She needed to shift back to heal, but without knowing the extent of the bullet wound, shifting back might make things worse. If the bullet was still inside, she could lose too much blood.

Again, just like Zac. By the time we'd found him, he couldn't control his shifts and had gone back and forth too many times. Lost too much blood. No healing power could've saved him.

My throat tightened. I couldn't lose Kali. Not now. Not ever.

From the corner of my eye, I caught figures running toward me. Rhett. A female close behind him. Clearly, they both thought ahead and stashed clothes nearby, unlike me. I didn't give a shit. My priority was healing Kali. My mate.

The female crouched on the other side of Kali's bear and moved to touch her wound.

I clutched her wrist. "What the fuck are you doing?"

Was that even my voice? It sounded too...raw.

Rhett placed a hand on my shoulder. "Layla's my daughter. She's a healer. Let her assess the injuries."

The name sounded familiar. Rhett had spoken of his daughter, of the pack's healer, but I'd never met her. While in Timber Falls, I kept to myself and Rhett respected that decision.

As much as it pained me, I nodded and released Layla's wrist. She leaned over Kali's bear, separating the fur around the bullet's entry point. Blood pooled on the mud beneath Kali, swirling with the rain in a horrific red river. My stomach rolled—so much blood.

Layla's gaze lifted to mine. "Can you carry her inside?"

I nodded. Numb. Completely fucking numb.

"Let me help," Harley said from behind me.

Crouching, I slipped my arms under Kali's upper body while Harley grabbed the bottom half. Together, we lifted Kali's bear into my arms. Thank God I grew up working on car engines. Lifting an adult bear required serious muscle, even if Kali was on the smaller side.

Once I settled her in my arms, Harley dashed ahead to the ranch. Kali's bear stirred and whined. I quickened my steps. Rain continued to pour, making me constantly adjust my hands so she didn't slip from my grasp. Wet hair plastered my face, but I focused on getting to the house. By the time I spotted it, my elbows locked into place and ached like a truck ran over them. Would they ever straighten?

As Harley reached the steps, Levi stumbled out the door onto the porch as though he'd just rolled out of bed. When his gaze caught mine, he snapped to attention, firing questions I couldn't answer. If I diverted my focus, I might drop Kali. Harley held the door open while Rhett darted ahead of me, straight to the kitchen, clearing a space on the table.

The moment I lowered Kali onto the table, Layla took over, demanding things left, right, and center. Whatever she requested, I gave her. No question asked. Thank fuck we regularly stocked the medical kit.

I wore a track in the kitchen floor as helplessness dug its way inside me, slowly killing my soul. At some point, someone handed me a pair of jeans and I slid them on.

I'd wasted so much time with Kali. Years where we could've been together, happy. I would've given her everything. Yet, when it mattered, I'd left. For what? Because I'd bruised my stupid ego? No, I exiled myself from this family because Kali deserved better. She still did. She deserved a mate who took care of her, protected her, offered her the fucking stars in the palms of his hands.

I'd promised to always protect her. But when she fucking needed me to, I wasn't here.

She bled out on that table because of me.

I clawed at my skull, twisting my fingers through my hair. Someone called my name. The voice sounded muffled, distant, barely audible.

I'd tried to coax Kali to shift for years, convinced she

was a shifter, but it never worked. In the end, the hurt behind her eyes every time it failed became too much. I gave up. Because I loved her for her, not because of what she might become.

After all this time, she'd shifted on her own. She didn't need me, she'd possessed the power all along. I was so wrong. Kali was never my weakness, she brought the best out of me, made me stronger. She gave me strength when I didn't know I needed it. And now she...

My bear whined, practically sulking in a dark corner. That made two of us.

"Brax?"

That voice again, this time closer. A gentle touch registered on my arm.

I lowered my hands. Layla stood in front of me. "You need to make her shift."

I peered at Layla's hand on my arm. Blood. A mixture of dark and light, dry and fresh. Kali's blood.

I searched Layla's eyes, trying to decipher her words.

They narrowed, hardened, filled with determination, reminding me of Kali. Her eyes did that every time she disagreed with something I'd said.

The hand on my arm squeezed. "Brax?"

I blinked a few times, clearing the wet film over my vision. "Is she...?"

I didn't know if I could survive without her. Who was I kidding? I knew, and the answer was no.

Layla lowered her hand and used it to coax me toward the table where Kali's bear lay, a blanket draped over her lower half. "Listen," Layla whispered. "Trust what you hear."

Inhaling a deep breath, I listened. And listened. What the hell was I meant to hear? With each breath, the whooshing in my ears faded, replaced with a faint, yet regular beat. Kali's heartbeat.

My knees buckled, and I clutched the edge of the table so I didn't collapse on the floor.

"You need to make her shift. She needs your blood."

A lump swelled in the back of my throat. Any of the shifters in this room could give her blood.

No. Fuck that. No way in hell I'd let someone else heal her. That was my job. Her mate.

But only an alpha had the power to make their pack shift. I wasn't the alpha of Cedar Valley. I gave up that birthright.

I peered over to Harley and Levi, standing in the doorway. "Harley?"

Harley's lips thinned into a tight line as he shook his head. "Alphas are born, Brax. You'll always be ours."

Levi tipped his chin. "I second that. There's only one alpha of this pack, and that's you, brother."

The weight of a big-ass boulder slammed onto my chest. Even after I'd abandoned them when Zac died, they still believed in me. Still considered me not only their brother, but their alpha. I'd never be worthy of their respect, yet in this moment, I wanted to be. This was where I belonged. Here in Cedar Valley. Here with my family and my mate. I still craved penance for all my failures, but maybe, just maybe, I could achieve that with my family by my side rather than without them. God knows, I'd fucking missed them. My soul hadn't been at peace since I left.

My damn throat closed, and I turned away before I did something really fucking manly like bawl my eyes out.

I stroked up and down Kali's fur, threading my fingers through the rough bristles. If I could, I'd give her those stars. I'd pluck every one of them from the night sky and capture them in a glass jar only for her. Hell, I'd bottle the entire universe if I could.

I'd do anything. But most of all, I wanted to be deserving of her love. I ached for her...forgiveness.

Closing my eyes, I mentally reached for the dormant alpha power flowing deep inside my blood. It sparked, awakened, and spread through my veins like an out-of-control wildfire, fueling my soul.

Drawing on the power, I whispered, "Shift."

A high-pitched whine sliced through my heart. Her bear jerked but didn't transform.

I couldn't lose her.

I leaned over Kali, splaying my hand over her heart. The faint beat was still there, but for how long? Lowering, I hovered my mouth against her ear. "C'mon, baby. Come back to me. *Shift.*"

I jumped back as Kali's bear jolted, shifting back into her human form in one swift movement. Relief nearly floored me. I adjusted the blanket to cover her better and pressed my lips on her clammy forehead. "I'm here, baby. You're going to be okay."

Someone handed me a knife. I didn't think twice. I sliced a thin line along my wrist and held it against Kali's lips. Blood pooled at the cut before seeping into her mouth. "Drink, Kal."

The blood dripped down her throat, but she didn't regain consciousness.

I glared at Layla. "It's not working. Why isn't she waking?"

Layla peeked beneath the blanket, inspecting the wound in Kali's abdomen. "Her body is in shock. The good news is the wound is healing. What she needs now is rest."

I nodded. Rest. I could give her that.

As the cut on my wrist sealed closed, I lowered my arm and scanned the room. I should thank people, especially Rhett. If he wasn't here, things with Jack Preston could've ended differently. But I couldn't find the words. All I wanted was to lay with Kali and hold her tight in my arms until she recovered. Until then, everything else could wait. "Can I move her to bed?"

With a soft smile, Layla nodded. "Of course."

Gently, I slid my arms beneath Kali's back and lifted to cradle her against my chest. Layla adjusted the blanket before stepping aside. On my way out of the kitchen, Harley squeezed my shoulder.

"It's good to have you home."

My chest swelled as words again caught in my throat. All I managed was a chin tip. No words encapsulated the love I felt for everyone in this room. Most of all for my mate, finally cradled in my arms where she belonged.

chapter nineteen

Kali

I peeled open my heavy eyelids to a golden hue spilling over my bed, cocooning me in a delicate layer of warmth. Blinking a few times, the fog swirling through my mind gradually thinned enough for me to identify the room. Brax's. How did I end up here?

Beside me, the bed dipped.

"Kal?"

I rolled my head toward his voice, too groggy and heavy to lift off the pillow as though I'd just woken from a deep slumber. Like for a year or so. Brax sat on the edge of the bed, concern etched on his beautiful face. All at once, the fog receded, and memories slammed into my mind. Particularly the one where I faced my father with a gun.

My head lolled back to stare at the ceiling. "Am I...dead?"

Every muscle in my body burned and ached, including ones I didn't know I had. But it didn't hurt. More like I'd rolled down a mountainside for shits and giggles, hitting every log and rock along the way and then took some wicked, life-altering painkillers. Beneath the achiness, a strange, almost primal power buzzed in my veins.

"I mean, I know I'm not dead-dead, but my body feels...weird. All warm and fuzzy, but at the same time...sore."

Brax's shuffled closer. "No. You're not dead. But you were lucky, Kal. So damn lucky. Rhett's healer removed the bullet and...my blood repaired the wound. The sutures fell out yesterday."

That explained the prickly sensation in my stomach. A bullet wound.

Asking about how he used his blood to heal me sounded bizarre. Did I drink it? Was his blood responsible for the strange buzz?

Hang on. Didn't I get to the gun first? "How did someone shoot me?"

Brax swept a cool, damp washcloth over my forehead making my shoulders sink further into the cushiony mattress. "From what we can piece together, you grabbed a gun, charged at your father as he...fired."

Clearly, trusting me with a gun wasn't a wise move. Note to self.

Bracing my palms on the mattress, I pushed into a sitting position. Everything felt strange.

"Let me help." Brax scooped his arms around me and lifted me, slipping a pillow between my shoulders and the headboard. "That better?"

I nodded. "Thanks. How long was I out?"

"Two days."

From the nightstand, he grabbed a glass of water and held it to my lips. I took a small tentative sip, testing the path down my throat. When the liquid arrived in my belly without incident, I took another. I tried not to scowl at him as he eased the glass away and placed it back on the nightstand.

So many fuzzy memories floated around in my mind that I struggled to make sense of them.

"Jack?"

Brax remained silent for a moment. "He's dead, Kal. A few of Rhett's pack...took him down. We buried what was left on the boundary as a warning to any hunters who traveled with him." Brax's hard gaze locked with mine. "Given how he threatened your life, not once, but twice, I have no regrets."

"Me either." That man was dead to me long before he attacked our home. I straightened, remembering Levi. "Is Levi okay? Jack stabbed him."

"He's fine. I presume you removed the knife?"

"If I didn't, he wouldn't have healed."

Brax's hand reached out but stilled before he touched my cheek. A faint pained expression flashed in his eyes as he lowered his arm back by his side. My chest tightened. Had I done something wrong? Was he angry with me for fighting my father? For abandoning Levi? Whatever troubled him caused a canyon to crack open between us.

"Thank you. You probably saved his life."

Without knowing how to respond, I chose silence, which then stretched between us so thick and heavy it turned awkward. I toyed with the frayed edge of the blanket draped over my legs.

"I think Jack thought I was here, and that Harley drove alone to the garage. He probably thought stabbing Levi would draw me out of the house." His voice became raw, roughened around the edges. "I should've stayed. I left you."

I lay my hand on his forearm, desperate to touch him —anything to lessen the distance growing between us. The last thing any of us needed was to shoulder more blame for the choices made by others. "My father attacked us, orchestrated this entire plan. You, *we,* did what any pack would do...protected our family."

When Brax didn't respond, that uneasy feeling intensified. Something was wrong. I'd never seen him this... haunted. Well, not since Zac died. Was he concerned I'd turn into a...Oh, no. That must be it.

Bile rose in my throat, and I slid my arm back under the covers. "If you gave me your blood, will I turn into a hunter?"

"No, Kal." He frowned, searching my eyes. "Do you remember what happened?"

An unfamiliar, strange sensation stirred in my head.

No, not stirred, *paced*. Followed by a growl only I heard. A bear growl. "Um...did I..."

"Shift?" His frown smoothed out. "Yeah. You sure as hell did."

"Huh."

Again, I didn't know what to say. Yay me? Ever since Zac first shifted, I'd wanted to, yearned to, but I never could. I'd resigned myself to the fact I wasn't a shifter. But now that I had, I wasn't sure how I felt. Would it even matter? I'd lived the last twenty-five years as though I wasn't.

"I guess with hunter and shifter parents, you could've become either one. Like Zac, your soul just needed a... trigger to shift."

That made sense. Zac had shifted for the first time when my father tried to kill me.

"Jack said Zac was an alpha. That he needed alpha blood to cure the hunter curse."

Brax nodded. "Dad suspected that's why he attacked you, to provoke Zac into shifting. But there's no evidence to suggest alpha blood cures the curse. No one's even heard of a hunter curing the curse once it's activated. I doubt it's even possible."

How many hunters were out killing alphas hoping for a cure that might not exist?

"He said he found us in Cedar Valley with your dad. Then he set this whole plan in motion just so he could get to you." I tried for my best amused smile, though it probably came across like a strained grimace. "Apparently you have some super powerful alpha blood."

Those jaw muscles tightened like crazy. "Apparently."

One question still plagued me though. "Shouldn't I have sensed somehow that my brother was an alpha? If I'm part shifter, albeit a very late bloomer, shouldn't I have sensed something like that?"

"Subconsciously you probably sensed it but put it down to him being your older brother."

Brax peered at the ceiling as though choosing his words. His chest expanded with a deep inhale before he glanced back at me.

"Kal, a shifter usually goes through their first change before adulthood. I assumed you weren't one. I'm sorry I didn't...help more."

"It's fine." I mean, what else could I say? That made sense. Without knowing my birth mother, I couldn't argue with his logic.

I stayed quiet for a few minutes, absorbing everything that had happened as distance once again crept between us even though he sat right beside me. In the space of a few days, our lives had flipped upside down. Had he changed his mind about leaving? Would he stay? Would we...I didn't even know what the situation was between us. We agreed to have sex, nothing more. But that was... before my heart took over and turned everything messy.

That all-consuming ache returned as other memories from the past week took front and center. We'd sealed our mate bond. But then he'd told me that he felt the same. Well, I didn't. Even now, with him sitting beside me, my soul sensed our connection in a way I couldn't explain. Did his blood amplify our connection? Was it one sided?

He'd told me our bond would seal if we had sex. At the time, I thought I couldn't feel more for him than I already did. But now he'd given me his blood and made it stronger. I felt his power coursing through my veins. Did he...regret using his blood to heal me? Was that it?

I didn't ask for his super fancy alpha blood. Sure, fine, I was glad he did, it clearly saved my life. But how could he be angry with me for that decision? Or was he angry with himself for doing something that strengthened our bond?

Beneath the covers, I twisted the sheet beside my hip as self-doubt did a mighty fine job overtaking my thoughts. When Brax first told me how he felt two years ago, he'd said it didn't matter whether I was a shifter, that he loved me for me. Then when Zac died, he left as though what was between us also didn't matter. I knew he left because of some self-inflicted punishment for failing his family, but still, he left. Whatever was between us wasn't enough to make him stay. Would knowing I was a shifter stop him from leaving again? That answer didn't matter. If he only wanted me because I was a shifter, then I wasn't okay with that. Was I not good enough as a standard human?

My fist clutched the blanket. If Brax still wanted to leave, fine. I wouldn't hold him back. I also wouldn't drag this out. I needed to know what happened now. If only, to prepare my heart. "So...Jack is dead. There's no longer a threat to the family...or me. I had my first shift, yay me. All is safe and well in Cedar Valley once again."

"Yeah. It's all over."

I tugged the blanket further up, creating a makeshift

protective shield for my heart. *It's all over.* Meaning...us? I'd allowed him into my heart long before my body. Honestly, I'd risk it all over again for Brax Archer. I always would. How stupid was that?

The sooner I finished this conversation, the sooner I commenced my mourning process. Otherwise known as bingeing on the carton of cookie dough ice cream in the freezer. That served me well last time.

"I guess that means you'll go back to Timber Falls?" I held his gaze, locking down the tears that threatened to break free.

He looked away and dragged his fingers through his messy hair. "Kal. About what I said when we..."

I held my breath aching for him to finish the sentence. To tell me he was wrong, that he wanted me. But...the words never came.

I bit the inside of my cheek, pulling myself together. I was stronger than this. I survived without him last time and I could do it again. "No need to explain. We were two adults who agreed to a morning of hot sex. You made it clear you wouldn't stay and I'm...fine."

God, the burn in my chest made my entire body ache anew. I relaxed my grip on the blanket before I tore it to shreds. Instead, opting to inspect the intricate stitching on the patchwork, the lumps in the material, the dark gray cotton, anything to distract me as I waited for Brax's reply.

"Is that...what you want? For me to leave?" His voice sounded rougher, deeper than a moment ago.

No, of course not. Not by a long shot. But if he truly

wanted me, he would've said it by now. He would've come home. He would've fought for me.

And...he didn't.

I had to let him go. He'd made it clear that after this threat was over, he'd go back to Timber Falls, and I'd stay here. I wouldn't hold him back because of some fated obligation and risk him resenting me for the rest of our lives.

No point avoiding the inevitable. Better to have loved and all that. What a stupid freaking saying. I wanted to punch the person who first said that in the face.

Lifting my chin, I summoned my last shred of self-preservation. "That's what we agreed."

Silence stretched between us for the longest time until it broke me. "It's fine, Brax. No hard feelings."

With a grunt, Brax stood and stormed out the door, slamming it shut behind him. When his footsteps faded down the stairs, I closed my eyes, allowing the tears I'd held back to stream down my cheeks like a never-ending waterfall. The last quarter of my heart shriveled up and died.

chapter twenty

Brax

How I kept the truck on the road was a fucking miracle. Both hands clutched the steering wheel, with my foot flat to the floor. Thank Christ the highway leading out of Cedar Valley was deserted, otherwise I would've crashed head-on into oncoming traffic. I barely had enough concentration for the road with all the shit running through my head.

Finally, I admitted my feelings for Kali, and she turned me away. Fine. I didn't admit it aloud, but I would've if she'd given me a chance. I'd tried to find the right words. How did I tell her that I was wrong? That all this time, I wished we'd been together. That after sealing our mate bond, my feelings for her had never been clearer. That I loved how my blood ran through her veins, drawing us even closer.

God, when Levi had called about Jack on the property, all I thought of was if something happened to Kali, I'd never forgive myself. That the second I saw her, I'd tell her how I felt, and we wouldn't waste another minute apart. But her recovery was my priority. Then, when I had the chance, I choked.

Me and my stupid fucking mouth. How I thought I'd leave Cedar Valley after sealing the bond with her, I'd never know. Such a dumbass move. Why did I even say that?

I accelerated more and the truck's engine whined. So long as the truck kept moving in the opposite direction to town, I didn't give a shit where I drove. I couldn't go back to Timber Falls. Not ever. I couldn't live in that town without her by my side and in my bed.

Each glance in the rearview mirror stabbed another dagger deep in my heart. I cranked up the music, blasting my eardrums, hoping to drown out the pain.

Without easing off the gas, I skidded around a bend almost daring the truck to crash—

A wolf darted onto the road. I slammed my foot on the brake, swerving in the opposite direction. Tires screeched off the road, chewing up dirt. The truck halted a mere foot before colliding with a tree.

My fists curled around the steering wheel while I sucked in gulps of air. Shit. That was close. And reckless.

Pull yourself together, Brax.

Wait a minute. I recognized that damn wolf.

I shoved open the driver's door and stormed out of the truck. Rhett waltzed across the road toward me. Buck naked.

"Are you fucking crazy?" I snapped at him. "I nearly hit you."

"Give me a bit more credit. My wolf is faster than your shitty truck."

I didn't have the patience for this conversation. Nor did I enjoy the idea of standing in front of Rhett with his dick hanging out for everyone to see, including me.

"Jesus." I leaned into the truck bed, snatched the blanket I always kept there and threw it at Rhett. "Cover that shit up."

Rhett wrapped it around his waist. "You heading somewhere in that feral mood?"

"I'm leaving. I don't belong there."

"Says who?"

I pointed down the road toward Cedar Valley, my voice as dark as my mood. "Says my mate who doesn't fucking want me."

Rhett remained silent, which just pissed me off. The man used it as a tactic, and I wanted none of that shit. Especially now.

"Did you run all this way to ask me that?" I growled, ready for this conversation to end.

"What do you want, Brax?" He narrowed his eyes. "Deep down, right where it hurts, what do you want?"

I shoved my fingers through my hair. I only ever wanted one thing, but I was too much of a coward to admit it. "I think that's fucking obvious, don't you?"

"Did you tell her? She's your mate you dipshit. Nothing rivals that bond. She shifted and took a bullet for you. Man the fuck up and tell her you're sorry."

If only life was that easy.

"All I've ever done is cause her pain. Her brother died because Jack fucking Preston wanted to kill me. Me," I shouted. "That asshole was so delusional he thought my blood could cure the hunter curse. Instead, he killed his own fucking son." My hands curled into fists. "She nearly died because I didn't protect her. And then I killed her father—"

"No."

Rhett stormed into my space and clutched my shoulder in a forceful grip.

"You listen to me, Brax Archer. I killed that piece of shit, not you. And I don't regret a single thing. That death isn't yours to shoulder. Nor is the death of your pack-mate. That asshole was a hunter, he killed his son, not you."

I stood there, glaring at Rhett while he glared back just as hard. He'd done that for me. Alpha to alpha. He killed Kali's father so I didn't have that death on my hands. I'd tortured myself enough over her brother's death. Adding more blood to the mix would send me spiraling out of control. If I hadn't already.

My throat tightened. I wanted to thank him, but how the hell did I say thank you for killing someone?

"Your father was the best, most honorable alpha I'd ever known. But I also had the pleasure of meeting your mother a time or two. That woman could rip me to shreds in a heartbeat with just a look." His grip on my shoulder softened. "The universe doesn't hand out mates on a production line. It grants us someone who will challenge us, who will make us better shifters, push us to become stronger alphas. Because without our mate, we're half a soul lost in the ether."

My mother always said the same.

Ever since I high-tailed it away from Cedar Valley, my bear had sulked in the background, but now it paced, huffing in agreement with Rhett. Again, where was the loyalty?

"Your folks didn't raise you to avoid taking the winding road because it was fucking long and treacherous. Being an alpha is hard. Life is even harder. But you know what, Brax?"

I met Rhett's steely pale blue gaze.

"We only get one shot at it. Are you going to waste it drowning in regret?"

Clarity seeped through the rage in my brain. I peered over Rhett's shoulder down the highway toward Cedar Valley. All I ever wanted was Kali Preston, and I never told her that. I'd never given her the chance to choose me. So caught up in self-pity, I never considered what we could become if I only gave us a chance. Protecting my pride was easier.

No more. That shit stopped now.

Rhett was right. Kali was my mate. I needed her. She made me stronger, called me on my bullshit, fought me tooth and nail when she disagreed with me or when I was being an ass. Whether she was a shifter never mattered to me. It still doesn't. My heart belonged to her, it bled without her. Two years ago I walked away because I thought she was better off without me. Now, I refused to give up without a fight.

Something in my look satisfied Rhett because he let go of my shoulder and stepped back with a shit-eating grin on his face.

"There. That's the alpha I knew you'd become. Now, go and grovel your ass off. Fight for your mate."

I needed that ass-kicking more than Rhett realized. More than I realized. "I..." I swallowed the lump lodged in the back of my throat. "Thanks, man."

He gave me a curt nod. Without another word, his body convulsed and shifted back into a wolf before darting into the forest out of sight.

Back in the truck, I hit the gas, turned around and sped down the highway, this time in the opposite direction. Back to Cedar Valley. Back to Kali. I just hoped she'd forgive me.

chapter twenty-one

Kali

I shoveled another giant spoonful of ice cream in my mouth. It tasted like glue. Once my brain stopped focusing on the massive gaping hole in my heart and realized cookie dough ice cream melted on my tongue, everything would improve.

I hoped.

Levi pulled out the chair across from me and sat. His spoon beelined for the carton.

"Back off, Levi." I scowled, jerking the ice cream out of his reach. "This is my comfort food. Get your own."

He scoffed. "That's _my_ ice cream."

I glared at him with all my inner badass bear. He did well to hold back his smirk. He grabbed a different carton from the freezer and returned to the table. Honeycomb. Brax's favorite.

For the love of all things junk food. Did he have to grab that flavor?

Cradling my ice cream in one hand, I kept shoveling that magical cure in my mouth. Sooner or later, it would work.

"I'm sorry, Kali. I really thought he'd stay."

Ice cream got stuck in my throat. I thought Brax would stay too. Even though he made it clear he wouldn't, that being alpha wasn't for him, part of me had still hoped he'd change his mind. Now, to go with my crushed heart, the memories of him kissing me, touching me, being inside me wouldn't cease their never-ending replay. That made everything hurt way more than last time.

I'd never recover from this.

I swallowed the tasteless ice cream. "It's fine. He made it clear he wouldn't stay. I'm fine." Kudos to me. My new mantra.

Levi raised a brow but lucky for him, he didn't argue. With my current mood, I'd probably claw his head off.

I tilted the carton and stared at the ice cream, hoping it turned into something more edible. Anything that took the pain away. Alcohol. Guys drowned their sorrows with alcohol. Maybe the ice cream needed a good splash of vodka on top.

No. Alcohol wasn't the solution, neither was ice cream.

I pushed the carton across the table to Levi. "Take it. It's not helping."

He popped the lids on and returned them to the freezer. "You're healed." He paused, frowning. "On the outside. Your bear is restless, Kali. You need to let her out for a run. That will help burn off some...frustration."

Frustration. More like anger, but I didn't correct him. The guy tried to make me feel better and I couldn't throw that back in his face. Not his fault Brax left. Again.

I threw my hands in the air. "I don't even know how to shift. This is all so new. I have no idea what I'm doing."

"I'll come with you. I'll show you what to do."

That hole in my chest split open further, swallowing my shriveled-up heart. "I don't want you to show me. I want..."

Brax. I wanted Brax. He'd promised to guide me if I ever shifted. He'd told me I wasn't alone. And yet...here I was.

I sagged into the chair. "And how will that help? It won't bring him back. I'm so stupid."

Harley strolled into the kitchen at the exact moment I commenced phase two of my emotional meltdown. The poor guy's face paled as his gaze darted between Levi and I, then he backed out the door. Brax's mom held me together when he left last time. She'd cradled my broken heart and told me everything would work out. Maybe I should visit her for a bit?

Truck tires skidded around the front of the house followed by a door slamming.

"Kali," Brax shouted.

I waved the spoon in the air. "Oh no, he doesn't. He

doesn't get to leave then come back and expect me to run into his arms just because he beckons."

Levi rolled his eyes. "You two are as stubborn as each other. No wonder fate paired you together."

I glared at Levi. "If he wants to talk to me, he can get down on his knees and beg."

He snatched the spoon from my hand and tossed it in the sink. "At least meet him halfway."

Of course he'd side with Brax. Damn brother loyalty.

"Fine." I shoved my chair back. "But no amount of groveling will fix this."

Before Levi said anything else, I strode out of the kitchen, threw open the front door, and stood on the porch with my hands on my hips. Brax waited on the path leading to the house.

"Brax Archer, if you're here to torment me some more I'm going to punch you in the face."

A smirk hinted at his lips which only infuriated me further.

He prowled closer, his gaze locked on mine. With each slow and determined stride, my stupid broken heart jolted to life. I didn't speak. More accurately, I couldn't. All that ice cream churned in my stomach anticipating what he'd say, why he came back. I couldn't allow myself to hope. That only led to eating my emotions.

He paused a few steps from the porch. "I still remember the first time we ever sat on these steps. It was the night Dad and I found you and Zac at that diner, and we took you in. You were so scared. We sat out here for hours, and I told you everything would be okay. I promised to always protect you and keep you safe."

He inched closer to the bottom step. "We sat here together on your fifteenth birthday and made wishes on the stars, then did it every year after that."

Oh, God. The memories clawed at my heart making it hard to breathe.

"I held you in my arms on that top step when that asshole stood you up for Prom. And you wouldn't let me take you instead until I promised not to rip the loser to pieces." Brax put one foot on the bottom step. His voice lowered. "We had our first kiss on these steps, and this is where I first realized I love you."

My pulse pounded in my ears and that churning in my stomach turned into flutters. Millions and millions of hopeful flutters. Somehow, without realizing, I glided closer.

"But there's one thing I haven't done on these steps. Something I should've done years ago." He ascended a few more until we were eye level. "I'm so fucking sorry. I was wrong to leave. This time and before. This is our home, Kal. You are my home. And I want to grow old with you here in this house."

From behind me, Levi cleared his throat.

Brax's gaze darted over my shoulder. "All right, smart ass." He took my hands in his, giving them a gentle squeeze. "I want forever in this house with you...and my two idiot brothers."

I couldn't breathe. What did he expect me to say? I'd wanted to hear those words for so long, they now didn't seem real.

"Kali Preston, I want to officially ask you, will you do me the honor of becoming my mate?"

I gasped. My heart stopped beating. The lid on my emotions exploded and tears pooled in my eyes. "But you said…"

He cupped my face in his strong hands and brushed the tears away using his thumbs.

"Sealing our bond didn't change how I felt. I already loved you more than life itself."

And there went my heart, fluttering away on a sparkly cloud.

"Are you sure this is what you want? Because I can't take you leaving again."

"Yes. I'm never leaving your side again. I don't wanna be anywhere without you, baby. I'm sorry it took me so fucking long to tell you that."

Levi was right. Brax and I were both stubborn. But the one thing we had in common was our love for each other. My heart would forever belong to Brax Archer. It always had.

"The suspense is killing me, Kal."

I chuckled. "Yes, I'll be your mate." I leaned closer, lowering my voice. "I already signed up for that."

His lip hitched on one side, and he guided me closer, crushing his mouth to mine, pouring his love through our kiss, mending my soul.

"About fucking time," Harley muttered behind us, totally ruining the moment.

I laughed. Brax wrapped his arms around my shoulders, holding me tight in one of his bear hugs. My mate gave the best hugs.

"Just so you know, you owe Levi a tub of ice cream," I murmured into his shirt. "It's your fault I ate it."

A chuckle rumbled in his chest. "Seems like fair payment."

He kissed the top of my head and I swear he smelled my hair again. Weirdo.

"I love you, Kal. And I plan to tell you that every goddamn minute until I'm worthy of your love in return."

I sighed a happy exhale. "You already are, Brax. I've loved you forever."

In that moment, my heart swelled, fusing back together, whole again for the first time in two years. Because finally we were both where we belonged. Together.

epilogue

Kali
One week later

I rehung some of my shirts in Brax's closet, straightening the non-existence creases in the sleeve. Technically it was *our* closet now, but it still felt strange saying that. Everything seemed so surreal. Brax was back in Cedar Valley, we were finally together, and I'd moved back into the Archer house.

Two years ago, I never would've imagined such a happy ending. Or our happy new beginning as Brax called it.

In the bathroom, I reorganized the vanity, making

sure my various skincare bottles didn't overtake the space. The bathroom was huge, even so, this girl sometimes went overboard with smelly lotions. Given Brax's weird obsession with smelling my hair, I'd forever keep the bottles fully stocked. Next, I straightened my toothbrush in the holder beside Brax's and stared at it for longer than I should have.

Warmth bloomed over my nape a second before Brax appeared in the doorway. He leaned a shoulder against the threshold and just looked at me. God, that man was downright sinful in a pair of jeans and a t-shirt, with his hair all scruffy and in need of a cut.

I moved my face cream slightly to the left. "Hey."

"You're stalling."

"Am not." *I totally am.*

He cocked a brow before pushing off the doorway to move closer. His earthy pine scent filled the air, sending shivers down my middle, exploding in a rush of heat between my legs. Recalling the wicked things he did to me in this bathroom last night only sent those tingles into overdrive.

Brax swept his knuckles over my jaw. "I'm right here, Kal. You're not alone."

My heart. I wish he'd stop making it a gooey mess. No, that was a lie. I loved how he thought he wasn't any good with words, yet always knew the right thing to say.

I sighed. I couldn't hide anything from him. "I just... what if I can't?"

He frowned before his brows smoothed out. Taking my hands in his, he lifted them to his chest. "You can, and you will. I believe in you."

There he went again, killing my heart with swoony words.

A week had passed since I first shifted when my father attacked, and I'd done everything possible to avoid shifting again. Not because I didn't want to, I did, but what if last week was a freak occurrence? What if I only shifted because Brax's life was in danger? What if it was some primal mate response to save him?

What if I couldn't do it again?

Letting one of my hands go, he tucked a wayward curl behind my ear. "Every shifter goes through this stage. The one where you're not sure how you shifted the first time. Where you doubt it's possible to do it again. Where your body doesn't know whether to embrace the sensations or puke."

I chuckled. Again, he knew me too well. Damn him.

"But baby, I know you can do it. A long time ago, I promised to help you shift and I intend to keep that promise."

I stared into his beautiful brown eyes, searching for a hint that he told me those words because I needed to hear them, not because they were the truth. I didn't find it. Only love reflected in his lingering gaze. Love with a dash of sexy alpha-ness.

I told him I'd try, yet day after day I found something else more important. Like moving into Brax's room or cleaning the apartment I no longer rented from Harley. I'd even found an excuse to grocery shop. And I hated grocery shopping with the fire of a thousand suns.

This morning when I woke warm and safe, cocooned

in Brax's arms, I had no more excuses. Today, I promised him I'd try and shift.

Tilting my head back, I peered up at him. "Okay."

He wrapped his arms around my shoulders, drawing me tight. "I'll be right here with you. I'm not going anywhere."

Maybe subconsciously I feared he would. Even though over the past week he'd proved to me he wouldn't leave, maybe part of me still worried that he might? What if I shifted, fully embraced this new life with him, and then something destroyed it?

What if this was the calm before the storm?

No. I wouldn't entertain those thoughts any longer. I'd vowed to stop thinking like that. Brax was here with me. We were together. I needed to live for our future, not in the past.

With a small nod, I let Brax lead me downstairs and out the back door. The house was unusually quiet for a Sunday. Levi and Harley must've gone into town while I hid up in Brax's room, reorganizing the closet for the umpteenth time.

Outside, Brax walked us to his truck, opening the door for me.

"We're driving somewhere? Can't I just shift here like you do?"

"Next time. For your first official shift, I want it to be somewhere special."

Ugh. Damn him. Why was he so growly on the outside, yet so soft and gooey in the center? I had no defense against that kind of swoon.

He rounded the truck, hopped in the driver's side,

and started the engine. I swallowed the lump in my throat and got in before I wimped out again.

As I sank into the passenger seat, Brax's phone pinged with a text. He checked it, replied, then dropped the cell in the door holder.

"Is everything okay?"

"Yep." He glanced at me. "Ready?"

I rolled my eyes. "As I'll ever be."

Brax laughed as the truck took off down the dirt road leading to the forest. A massive swarm of winged creatures took flight in my stomach. My mouth went dry. My heart raced so fast, Brax could probably hear it thumping from the driver's seat. To avoid puking all over the dash, I distracted myself trying to guess where he was taking me.

Before long, Brax entered the forest, and giant pines caved in all around us. I loved this part of the world, this forest, the Archer estate. Reaching over, Brax took my hand in his, sending a wave of calm through our bond. God, I loved him more and more each day.

After a few minutes, he steered the truck off the main road, onto a dirt track. I couldn't stop the smile from warming my face. Although I hadn't been here for what felt like forever, I'd never forget the way.

Brax squeezed my hand, somehow sensing my thoughts. "I figured you'd feel more comfortable here."

The truck exited the thick forest, arriving at a clearing by a river. Afternoon sunlight sparkled off the crystal-clear water, giant mountains loomed in the distance, the sound of water rushing over rocks calmed my racing pulse.

Hopping out of the truck, I stood there for a moment

with my eyes closed, breathing a deep breath of fresh, crisp air. The kind only found here.

Brax snaked his arms around my waist, resting his chin on my shoulder. "I still remember the first day I brought you here. Mom and Dad had thrown that big welcome party for you and Zac at our house and invited the neighboring shifters, but you felt so overwhelmed you hid in your bedroom."

I chuckled at the memory and twisted to face him. "And you rescued me by sneaking us out the back door. It took us forever to walk here."

"Worth every step." He glanced at the river, his gaze lost in thought. "I knew that day."

I frowned. "Knew what?"

He tucked another curl behind my ear. "I knew you were my mate. I don't think I fully understood the feeling, but I knew there was something magical between us. And in that moment, I knew I'd do anything for you."

Lifting on my tippy-toes, I pressed my lips against his. What started out as a gentle, innocent kiss quickly intensified. Brax angled my head to deepen our kiss, sweeping his tongue over mine. My entire body heated as I surrendered to the sensations streaming through our bond.

Love. Awe. Hope.

Slipping my hands beneath his shirt, I smoothed them over his taut back muscles as they clenched and rippled beneath my touch. Brax moaned, maneuvering us to press my back against the truck.

With a growl, he eased back, still cradling my face in his palms. He rested his forehead against mine.

"As much as I want you naked right now in the bed of

my truck, we came here for a reason."

"I kind of hoped kissing you would make you forget that minor detail."

He laughed, stepping back. "Nice try, Kal."

I couldn't avoid it forever. "Okay, how do I do this? Ask my bear to...appear?"

Lucky for him, Brax held back his smirk. "Sort of. Do you feel that strange sensation in your mind? Like another being is in there with you?"

I nodded.

Brax took my hand, leading me away from the truck. Probably so I didn't accidentally claw it apart. "Good. Now close your eyes and focus on the feeling. Surrender to it. Embrace your shifter half."

I did as he instructed, waiting for the next step. Surely, there was more to it than just embracing my bear side.

When he said nothing else, I opened my eyes. "That's it?"

He nodded. "You can do it, baby."

"Right. Okay."

I closed my eyes again and focused on the niggling sensation in the back of my mind. The strange feeling swelled inside me, building, and intensifying until it... consumed me. As though it took control of my body on a molecular level. Slight tremors quaked through my middle, becoming stronger and more frequent. Images flashed through my mind—Brax, his bear...my bear. My back bowed. A rush of heat exploded in my center as a growl rumbled from my chest.

I panicked, snapping open my eyes.

"I'm right here, Kal," Brax whispered, just before darkness overtook my vision.

I came to buck naked on my knees in the dirt at the base of a giant tree. Icy water dripped down my back from my wet hair. How the hell did I get my hair wet? In a rush, snippets of memories flashed in my mind. *Shifting into a bear...Brax walking beside me, leading me through the forest...him shifting...his bear coaxing me into the river... splashing and playing without a care in the world.*

I tucked my arms around my legs, huddling in a ball. Despite shivering, I couldn't wipe the smile off my face.

A warm blanket wrapped around my shoulders a second before Brax crouched beside me, fully dressed. Clearly, he shifted back before me. "How do you feel?"

"That was, hands down, the coolest thing I've ever done."

He beamed with pride as he wrapped his arm around my shoulders.

"Does it always feel like that?"

"You get used to it over time, but yeah, there's always a rush. A sense of freedom."

Freedom. That was it. I felt free.

Offering his palm, Brax helped me to stand. A dull ache lingered over my body as though I'd rediscovered muscles I hadn't used since last week. By the time we reached the truck, the sun dipped behind the mountain, streaking deep pink and orange across the sky. The first stars were just visible above the horizon.

I gaped at the shredded fabric on the ground. "I forgot to take my clothes off before I shifted. Rookie mistake."

Brax reached into the truck's bed and grabbed a bag, handing it to me. "I brought you spare clothes and a towel. I thought we could spend the night at the cabin."

That man thought of everything. Alone time sounded like a damn good idea.

I dried my hair first, then unzipped the duffle bag. "How often do I need to shift?"

"Whenever you feel the urge. Your bear will let you know."

I pinched a lacy black thong between my fingers and waved it in the air in front of his face. "Really?"

He lifted one shoulder. "It's my favorite."

I rolled my eyes, quickly dressing before I died of hypothermia. Okay, fine, I wasn't that cold, but it was far from warm. While I dressed, Brax checked his phone again. And again. He'd checked it three times in the past few minutes.

"Is something wrong?"

He tucked the phone in his back pocket. "Nope. We're just...a little late for something."

"Late? For what?"

He kissed my forehead and threw the duffle bag in the truck. "Something."

On the way back, I couldn't stop replaying the memories in my mind. Why was I so scared to shift? Brax had promised to help me, he'd assured me he'd be there the entire time and he'd done exactly that.

Was I officially a shifter now? I'd shifted into a bear

with no major trigger or life-threatening situation. I'd done it all on my own. It seemed like a turning point in not just my life, but for Brax and I. As though we could both finally embrace who we were born to be.

Brax parked the truck at the back of the house. But instead of going inside, he took my hand and led me along the wrap-around porch toward the front. Just before we rounded the corner, he turned to me, lifting my hand to place a gentle kiss on the inside of my palm.

"Before things get crazy, I want to tell you how proud I am of you shifting today even though the thought terrified you."

"I wouldn't say terrified."

He cocked a brow.

Fine. It totally did.

Hang on. "Before things get crazy? What are you up to, Brax Archer?"

He smirked. "You'll see."

If I didn't know better, I'd say the poor guy was nervous by the way his gaze kept darting around the corner. Which, of course, made those winged creatures return to my belly.

After a lingering gaze, Brax walked me around to the front porch.

My breath hitched.

"Surprise," he whispered.

I couldn't reply. I couldn't even move. The scene on the front lawn stole every ounce of my breath.

Someone had strung hundreds and hundreds of fairy lights in the air between the trees. Glass lanterns with tea light candles flickered over the lawn, on tables, and hung from branches. The yard looked as though all the stars in the universe had descended from the night sky to hover over this patch of lawn.

Under the lights, food and drinks covered the tables, people mingled, chatting to one another. I spotted Levi and Harley, plus Rhett and his daughter Layla. Other faces looked familiar from neighboring packs, but I couldn't remember their names. My heart skipped when I noticed the long burgundy carpet rolled out at one side of the gathering. A guy stood at the edge with his hands clasped in front of him, waiting.

I recognized that guy from when neighboring packs invited the Archer family to...

"A mating ceremony."

Brax pulled me closer, squeezing my hands. "I'm not good with words, Kal. But I wanted to show you how much you mean to me. You're my entire universe, and I want you to have all of me in return. My heart, my body, my soul. And my name."

Tears blurred my vision.

"When I told you I'm never leaving you again, I meant it. I want to make it official. I want the world to know I'm yours and you're mine. I'll probably still screw things up along the way, but I've wasted so much time. I don't want to waste another second."

He cupped my cheeks in his hands. I lost myself in his dark brown eyes, in the love and adoration reflected from deep within his soul.

"Kali Preston, will you do me the honor of officially becoming my mate?"

I glanced to the people gathered on the lawn who'd

stopped talking to watch the scene between Brax and I unfold. Brax's mom stepped forward, catching my eye. She smiled and something swelled inside my heart until it almost exploded right there on the porch.

"Your mom's here."

He kissed my forehead. "I flew her back for the ceremony. She's going to visit for a few days."

"What if I say no?"

He didn't skip a beat. "I'll ask you again tomorrow. And the day after that. I'll ask you every day until you say yes."

He'd organized this entire night to show me how much he loved me, his commitment to us, how he intended to stay.

I peered up at Brax, and all my doubts flew away with the breeze.

He was right. We'd wasted so much time already and I wanted to embrace our future.

"Yes, Brax Archer. I'll officially become your mate." I playfully smacked his chest. "I wish you packed me something nicer to wear."

"I did." A sinful smirk curled on his mouth. "But that's for later tonight."

I couldn't contain my smile. "God, I love you."

His eyes heated, sparking with mischief. "Show me."

Curling my hands around the back of his neck, I pulled him down and took his mouth in a scorching kiss, not fit for an audience. Cheers and claps rang out from the lawn, but I didn't care. I'd never felt so whole, so complete, so loved. I loved this man with all my heart, and I couldn't wait to spend the rest of our lives together.

Craving more small-town shifters? Grab your copy of **Salvation** and discover where it all began, or preorder **Awaken** and swoon over the Wolves of Timber Falls coming in 2022.

ALSO BY CASSIE LAELYN

The Fallen Guardians

Unforsaken (Book 1)

Unforgotten (Book 2)

Unseen (Book 3)

Untamed (Book 4) coming 2021!

Small Town Packs

Salvation

Reclaim

Awaken (coming soon!)

ABOUT THE AUTHOR

Cassie is an award-winning paranormal romance author living in sunny Queensland, Australia with her husband and two BMX-crazy boys.

She has a passion for crafting stories involving loyal, otherworldly characters in need of love and redemption. She's also a self-confessed chocoholic and a huge sucker for an angsty, gut-wrenching happily ever after.

When she isn't narrating imaginary characters, Cassie loves binging on TV shows, spending time at the beach, and curling up listening to the rain.

Join Cassie's newsletter (www.cassielaelyn.com) to stay up to date with release information, including the next instalment in her award-winning, steamy paranormal romance series, The Fallen Guardians.

You can also stalk @cassielaelyn

Facebook ~ Instagram ~ Twitter
BookBub ~ Goodreads